REDEMPTION

BLACK HOODS MC #6

Dark Redemption

For him, Sturgis Motorcycle Rally is like heaven on earth. For her, it's a living hell.

Jonas "TwatKnot" Murphy descends on Sturgis with a fairly simple plan.

1. Drink his weight in alcohol.

2. Get laid.

3. Live Bike Week to the fullest.

Offending the curvaceous bartender was not on that list. Nor was chasing after her to apologize. But she's under his skin now, and even her smart mouth won't stop him now.

Cora Jean Webb hates Bike Week, and as far as she's concerned, TwatKnot can shove his apology and his stupid sexy man bun where the sun don't shine. After what he had said, it doesn't matter that he's the hottest man she's ever seen or makes her feel alive again.

Then trouble rides back into town and Cora must make a choice between her safety or her bruised heart.

To the real life Greta Titsworth.

And her great set of melons.

Love you!

TWATKNOT

STURGIS FUCKING SOUTH DAKOTA, home to the world's largest biker rally. Ten days filled with endless debauchery, concerts, bikes, and pussy. The closest thing to heaven for a guy like me, and it's all mine to conquer.

I take in the scene around me under the hot rays of the summer sun. Grassy fields where tents and RVs of all shapes, sizes, and colors fill every possible space. The roar of hundreds of motorcycles almost drown out the music blaring from the pavilion to our left, where a shitty rock band is playing. The good bands won't be here until later in the week, but even the shitty ones add to the spirit of the rally.

Throwing out my arms, I holler, "Daddy's fucking home, baby!"

"I'm *not* calling you Daddy, fucker," I hear from over

my shoulder. I turn to see Priest sneering, fumbling with the poles to his tent. "Fucking piece of shit."

What should be a five-minute setup is now going on twenty. I would've been finished with mine already, but watching V and him struggle is way too much fun. Rookies, the both of them. I tried telling them to put it up before we left so they'd know how to put it together, and not look like complete dumbasses in front of the ladies. Obviously, neither of them listened.

All he has to do is ask for help, but he's a stubborn asshole.

"Need a hand over there, boy scout?" I laugh, but all he does is glare at me.

I wonder if he ever looked at the nuns like that? Hell, maybe it was his smoldering looks, melting the nuns' panties that caused him to leave the church. All I know is that one of these days, I'll get him to tell me why he left it to join our club. Though he's been tight-lipped about it all, I'm pretty sure GP might know his story, but he's an even tougher nut to crack. Maybe when I catch one of them nice and relaxed, they'll let it slip… with the help of a few bottles of whiskey, of course.

Bending down, he grabs two of the poles. Once they're connected, he attempts to insert it into the tent's sleeve, all the while holding the instructions in the same hand. Then halfway through, the pole comes apart.

"Motherfucker!"

"Language, Father," I tease.

"Fuck you, man," he growls, flinging the tent to the ground. "Tell me again why the club is at the Holiday Inn, sleeping on beds in air-conditioned rooms, while we're roughing it out here in Satan's ass crack?"

The old ladies are the reason the guys aren't here and are at the hotel, which is fine by me. It just means more beer and pussy for the rest of us.

"The experience," I say matter-of-fact. "This is your first rally, and you'd be doing yourself a disservice by not experiencing it the way it was meant to be. You need to see it like I did for the first time." Damn, those are some great memories. "This is Sturgis central, where all the good shit happens. It's not in town or on Main Street —it's right here."

It's been years since we've made the trek up here from Texas. After all the shit we've been through, this trip is just what we needed. A chance to relax and take a load off from all bullshit back home. Well, for some of us, anyway. With GP's old lady knocked up, he wasn't about to take off and leave her to help watch all the brothers' kids. Between the two of them and Mom, who'd also signed up for babysitting duty, they'd be having a different kind of experience all together. Our club has gone from brotherhood to motherhood in a fucking flash. Not that I mind having the ladies around, or the kids, but shit's changed fast.

"What, like loose pussy and STD tests?"

Trudging over to his pile of shit, V tosses his bedroll down on his tent bag with a huff. "I didn't know a week of back pain and listening to you fuck around classified as an experience. Did they make you do this your first time up here as punishment? Because that's exactly what this feels like. I'm a patch, remember? This is prospect shit." V continues cussing up a storm while trying to get his tent out of the storage bag.

"Judge can always take the patch back, ya know?"

He flips me off, but I shake my head and smile. They have no idea what's coming their way this week. They're bitching now, but when we make it out on the town tonight, they'll thank me.

"You two gonna bitch and moan the whole trip?"

"Yes," they answer in unison. Fucking pussies.

Ignoring them, I finish up my tent. The sooner we get this shit done, the sooner we can get to the bars, and I plan on having a great fucking time, unlike these two dipshits.

Stuffing my bedroll and supplies into my new polyester home, my attention gets drawn elsewhere when a stacked little blonde with a big, juicy ass sashays by our spot. Those round cakes of hers look primed for someone like me to take a big fucking bite out of. And that little smirk she's sending my way tells me all I need to know, that I'm the kind of guy she's looking to play with, and

I'll happily oblige her. She stops and watches me until the two jackasses arguing over what goes where.

"It goes in slot B," V argues, shoving the instructions into Priest's face.

"Fuck that. It goes into slot A…" His words trail off when he spies our onlooker. Both go silent and their bodies grow stiff. *Yeah, that's right. Now you know what I'm talkin' about, boys.*

"You see what I'm seeing?" Priest asks V.

"Yup," he responds. "Is she looking at you or me?" V runs his fingers through his hair like a bashful fucking teenager, and it takes everything I have not to laugh out loud. I mean, seriously? Between the three of us, if a woman like that is picking either of those two over me, Hell would have to be freezing over.

"Jesus," I mutter. "You two are nuttin' in your jeans at the first pretty little thing that walks by." I wave at the blonde, watching a rosy blush fill her cheeks as she waves back and continues on her way, leaving the three of us watching her go. "And she was looking at me, in case you didn't notice."

"The fuck she was," V argues.

"Girls like her are a dime a dozen up here, boys. You just have to pick the age, shape, and cup size." I cup my hands and bring them up to my chest. "Just wait till we hit up the bars tonight. And speaking of which, if you two ladies will finish up with your housework, we'd be there already with the guys, so how about that help now? I'd like to get to the Moose Knuckle before all the good pussy is snatched up."

"Fuck it. Fine, help us," Priest relents. V tries to hand me the instructions, but I shove his hand away.

"I don't need that shit. Shoving a steel rod into a tight hole is my specialty," I chuckle. "Here, let *Daddy* show you how it's done."

CORA

"HEY, sweet cheeks. How 'bout another round over here?"

I nod to the burly biker a few feet to my right, letting him know I heard him, and finish the drink order I'm working on. The music is pounding, and the strobe lights are giving me a headache. Every square inch of the place is filled with bikers, half-naked women, and the line for drinks is three rows deep.

Welcome to the Moose Knuckle Tavern during the first night of Bike Week here in Sturgis.

I fucking hate bike week.

Every year, I take this week off and head over to Omaha to visit my Aunt Shirley. But this year, Carl, the owner of the Moose Knuckle Tavern, and therefore my boss, rolled his motorcycle three days before the rally was set to start, which left me with no choice but to take over the tavern while he lies in bed, his leg in a cast from hip to toe, and a road rash I imagine hurts like hell.

"Honey, over here!" someone calls out from my left.

Taking a deep, not-so-cleansing breath, I plaster on a smile and wave to acknowledge the man. *Where the fuck is Stella?*

Stella's the part-time bartender Carl had hired to help out this week, but things aren't going so well. She's constantly taking breaks and is never on time. Last night, I found her in Carl's office, bent over his desk, getting nailed by some smelly biker with a beer gut and a cigarette dangling from between his lips.

I whip out a few more orders and finally turn my attention to the guy on my left. The instant my eyes land on him, the air is sucked straight out of my lungs. Hell, I'm pretty sure my vagina just quivered with excitement. *Who knew it could even do that?*

"Hello, gorgeous," he purrs, flashing a smile that could melt every female heart in this room, except for mine.

"What can I get ya?"

Mr. Too-Sexy-To-Be-A-Biker places a twenty on the bar top and winks. "A Skinny Bitch."

Fury flows through me like molten lava. Narrowing my eyes, I press my hands on the counter and lean forward. "Listen up, fuckface. Just because you have an asshole, doesn't mean you have to be one. Now, what do you want to drink?"

Roars of laughter come from the group of men standing directly behind him, but he doesn't laugh or look pissed. Instead, he looks shell-shocked, his face white beneath that delicious beard. His mouth is open in surprise, and his eyes are wide.

This is just one of the many reasons I fucking hate bike week. These fuckers think they can talk to women like they're shit and stomp all over their feelings and their hearts. But you can't stomp on a heart that's not available. As for my feelings, they may get hurt, but I'll never give them the satisfaction of knowing it.

I've always been a curvy girl, and seeing as I don't plan on starving myself or breaking my back at a gym, I probably always will be. And I'm good with that, because I think I look good. I'm also a nice person who treats people with kindness and respect, and I go to church on Sundays. I won't change any of that just to be treated as eye candy for the likes of this doofus with the stupid twat knot/man bun on top of his head.

"I—" he sputters. "I didn't… That's what I want to drink—a Skinny Bitch. Vodka, soda, lime?"

Oh. My. God. If I could crawl under the bar right now and disappear, I'd do it.

"Right," I chirp, quickly grabbing a tumbler from the tray of clean glasses. My hands tremble with embarrassment as I make his drink, all while feeling his eyes on me.

I turn and place the glass on a napkin in front of him, unable to meet his eyes. "I apologize," I say, raising my voice to be heard over the deafening combination of music and laughter. "I thought..." I snap my mouth shut and shake my head. I'd thought he was calling me fat, and now I look like an idiot. "Anyway, enjoy your drink."

I pull away and move on to the next person in line, trying desperately to ignore the feel of his gaze on me as I work. He's probably wondering how I'm here behind the bar without a keeper, because clearly, I must be insane.

I can't help but sneak glances at him from the corner of my eye as I move behind the bar. He's beautiful. Chiseled muscles. Blond hair pulled into a bun at the back of his head. I normally hate that look, but on this guy, it makes my ovaries do a little flip inside my otherwise neglected lady parts.

"Another one, sweetheart?"

Keep it together, Cora. He's just a guy, and a biker guy to boot. You don't like bikers, remember?

Placing his drink in front of him, I move to take the bill clamped between his fingers, but he holds it tight. I look up and freeze instantly. His electric blue eyes hold me captive, sending jolts of electricity buzzing throughout my body.

"I hope you know I wasn't being an asshole." The sincerity in his gaze makes my knees weaken even more.

"Yeah, sorry about that. I've just never had a man order that before, and—"

"That's 'cause our boy here's a giant vagina in training." A massive tattooed arm wraps around him from behind. "Ain't that right, TK?" the guy chuckles. "He likes ladies' drinks. Hell, he even does his hair like a lady. Makes you wonder how he thinks he can please one, doesn't it?"

TK sneers and shoves his buddy away. "Fuck you, Karma." Releasing the money from between his fingers, he turns his attention back to me. "Ignore him. He's got a big mouth and a small dick."

I place his change on the bar top. "You sound like you're pretty familiar with his dick."

Karma barks out a laugh, and TK smiles.

Just then, a pretty blonde girl with fake tits and too much make-up slides in between TK and the bar. Her long, tanned arms come up and wrap around his neck, instantly reminding me of where I am and who this guy is. I turn on my heel and get back to work, not wanting to see what happens next.

I fucking hate bike week.

TWATKNOT

THE SMELL of cheap whiskey and perfume fills my nostrils when I wake to an ass wiggling against my cock. My eyes strain to open, and when they do, I find the pretty little blonde from the bar last night with the voluptuous ass pressed up against me. I shake my head, trying to clear the looming hangover pounding inside of my skull. The blonde—whose name I don't remember—continues to wiggle. *Shit, she's awake.* Normally, I'd cut and run before the sun was up, but that's a little hard to do when this is my tent. If I want to get out of here, I'll have to get creative.

"Morning," she purrs, peering over her shoulder at me under those thick, fake eyelashes. "Last night was fun."

I smile. "It was." Most of what I remember was fun, anyway. My cock buried in that sweet ass of hers, and the way she screamed like a porn star as I fucked her. V and Priest were beating on the side of the tent, telling me to shut her the hell up. Good night all in all, except for that run-in with the mouthy, yet intriguing bartender at the Moose Knuckle.

"Want to get some breakfast?" she asks, pulling me back to my current predicament of getting her out of here. "I know a little place close by."

Warning lights go off in my head. Blondie here doesn't understand this was a one-night only party for two that's meant to end by the time the sun rises.

"Listen, sweetheart, last night was fun, but that's all it was—fun, for the both of us." I go to move away from her, but I don't get far. My naked back hits the slick fabric, stopping me from going any farther.

I almost flinch when her face flushes with embarrassment. "Oh."

"It's nothing against you. You're fucking hot, but I'm here for a good time. You understand, don't you?"

"Yeah, sure." Huffing, she gets to her knees and starts searching for her clothes. Seeing her bra in the corner, I snag it off the floor and hand it to her, only to watch her hold it against her chest like she's suddenly shy.

It wouldn't be this weird if she understood the assignment. At no point did I let on that I was looking for a commitment. It's bike week. She knows what it is, or she should.

As soon as she finishes gathering her things, she bolts from the tent without another word.

Stepping out behind her, I find V and Priest staring at her naked ass walking away in a huff. Their eyes shift to me and I look away.

"Lover's quarrel?"

"Some women get it, some don't. Didn't put two and two together that she was a patch bunny looking to be adopted." I stretch my arms out over my head, trying to work out the kink in my shoulder. Priest's eyes go wide when he looks over in my direction.

"Dude, put on some fucking pants."

I look down and shrug. "Don't be jealous, boy scout. Not everyone can be this lucky."

"You're lucky it hasn't fallen off, dickhead."

Reaching back inside the tent, I grab my jeans and tug them on.

"There, I'm dressed." I notice the bags under their eyes. "You ladies don't look like you got much sleep."

"No shit, Sherlock. Between her screaming and your snoring," Priest growls, "I got exactly zero hours of sleep."

"Aw, you poor babies."

"You at least owe us some fucking breakfast."

"A big one," V adds.

"You've already seen a big one this morning." I shift my gaze down to my crotch and roll my hips. "Bet it's the biggest you've ever seen, too. Hell, it's shaping up to be a big week for you guys already."

V looks ready to hit me. "Not your dick, fuckface. I'm talking steak, eggs, fucking pancakes with syrup that has real blueberries in it, not that artificial shit." He continues to list out six more breakfast items before I finally stop him.

"Sure thing. It's the least I can do." I smile, knowing damn well we're meeting up with the guys for breakfast on the club's dime. "Let me get my shit and we can get that breakfast you're bitching about."

I step through the flap to get a clean shirt from my duffle. Sliding it over my head, I finish off my morning care routine with some deodorant and body spray. I'd already made plans to swing by one of the guys' rooms later for a shower, because there's no way in hell I'm using the ones setup at the campground. I draw the line in the sand over that experience. I'd seen enough shit go down in those stalls that would last me a lifetime.

Grabbing my phone off the solar charger, I head back outside and find V and Priest waiting on their bikes. Peering down at my phone, I realize why. We were supposed to meet the brothers at nine, and it's fifteen after. Shit.

I slide my leg over the cool, black metal tank, still wet from the morning dew. The only time this place is remotely decent this time of year is in the morning, so we have to make the best of it before the blistering mid-day sun starts warming the place up like a brick oven. The engine on my bike roars to life as soon as I hit the ignition switch. V and Priest take off toward the main part of town, and I follow behind them.

Every street is packed with bikes—old, new, and modified. We get lucky and spy a group of men pulling out of their spaces just a few blocks away from the restaurant Judge had picked out the night before. As soon as we get parked, we step inside the packed fucking dining room. The noise level is off the charts, but a loud-ass whistle draws my attention to the brothers, tucked into one of the large tables in the back, flanked by their old ladies in cuts that match our own. Judge is sitting there, arms crossed, with Grace tucked in close to his side. His glare intensifies the closer I get to the table.

"You forget how to tell time after getting patched?" Judge quips.

"TK had to get his dick out of that blonde chic, Prez."

Judge's mouth turns up in a tight smile. "Figured as much."

We head toward the end of the table, where a few open seats remain. V and Priest end up next to each other at the very end, but I force my way in next to Lindsey, much to Karma's displeasure. Settling in, I pick up the menu and look over the basic breakfast shit, and even I have to admit, I worked up quite an appetite.

Might regret it later with this hangover, but a man has to eat.

An older waitress comes over to take our orders. Honestly, with as busy as this place is, I'll be lucky to get my food before lunch. That's when I spy a lonely piece of bacon on Lindsey's plate next to me, ripe for the taking.

"Morning, sugar tits," I drawl, warming up for the distraction.

"Sugar tits?" Karma growls from the other side of her. "The fuck you just call my woman?"

My plan is working.

"Calm down, big guy. Just saying hello to my favorite girl."

He starts to reach over to deck me, but Lindsey elbows him in the ribs. "I can take care of myself, you know." With her eyes focused on him, and his now focused on her, I go to nab that piece of bacon when a fork comes down dangerously close to my thumb. A fork attached to StoneFace's monstrous hand.

The impact draws Lindsey's attention back to her plate. When she realizes what I was trying to do, she looks up and sneers at me, but all I can do is smile innocently.

"Back off my bacon, asshole. If you'd have gotten here on time, you too might have some hot, crispy, savory bacon." Closing her eyes, she brings the piece to her lips and takes a bite. "Mmm, delicious," she moans seductively.

"Unlike your man, I share," I grumble. "Sharing *is* caring." Quick, I try to snatch the bacon from her fingers, but she jerks it away.

Karma smirks. "She ain't sharin' shit with you, dickface."

"Karma says no sharing, so no sharing." She takes another bite and chews it slowly, watching me out of the corner of her eye. She does this until it's gone, then gives me a wide smile when Karma pulls her closer to him, as well as her plate.

As much as I like to tease the ladies, I'm not a dumbass. I know messing with them is also messing with my brothers, but it's just so much fun stirring the pot, especially when it's Karma. Pressing his buttons is pretty much my specialty. All the shit I took from him as a prospect, I'm giving back to him little by little. And now, with Lindsey officially his girl, it's way too damn easy to rile him up, and I never pass up an opportunity to do so.

"What happened to you last night?" StoneFace asks from my left.

"Had a little business to take care of."

"His *business* was giving it to the blonde that followed him around like a lost puppy at the bar," V chimes in. "Trust me, her moans are burned into my memory."

"Happy to give you your first memorable Sturgis experience, bud. I'll try to make some more for you later tonight."

V glares at me.

"Don't mind him. He's just a little grumpy 'cause he didn't get any sleep."

Judge rolls his eyes at me from the end of the table. "There are still a couple of open rooms at the motel," he reminds V and Priest.

"And rob them of the experience, Prez? Come on, now. They'll appreciate it later."

"More like, I'll smother you in your sleep," Priest mumbles under his breath.

"Oh, that's a sin, Father. You don't want any dark marks on your record," I chuckle. "How many Hail Marys will you have to say for that again?"

He starts to say something, but the waitress arrives with our food in tow. The greasy goodness on my plate is going to wreak havoc on my body later, but I don't give two shits right now. Bacon shits, be damned. I devour it all in record time, while the rest of the group sits and chats like a bunch of old women at their crocheting clubs.

When we're all finally finished, Judge snatches the bill from the waitress, and Priest and V take notice.

"Don't think you're getting out of owing us a big breakfast, dickhead."

I snort. "You didn't say I had to pay for it."

"So what's on the schedule for today, Prez?" Hashtag asks over the crowd.

"I have to head into a meeting with all the chapter presidents."

Grace frowns. "Meeting?"

"Just a formality. Shouldn't take too long," he responds vaguely, but the guys know what he means. With so many clubs here for bike week, ground rules must be made. Concessions on any beef happening between clubs cease while we're here on neutral ground. Violating those rules would come with heavy consequences for anyone involved, including losing your patch. As National President of The Black Hoods MC, Judge must attend.

"I thought us girls could hit up some of the local shops," Shelby, Hashtag's ol' lady, mentions, with all women chiming their agreement. Thankfully, with all of them wearing their property patches, their guys shouldn't have to worry too much about them getting into any trouble. But seeing the look on Judge's face tells me one of us will be tagging along. He looks over the crowd before his eyes land on me.

"Oh, fuck no," I argue before he even asks. "Don't make me go."

"You're going," Judge orders with a smile. "If you'd

shown up on time, I might've asked someone else, but today's your lucky day, TK."

"Fine," I scoff, because there's no point in arguing with him. When the president says to do something, you do it, no matter how much you hate it. "But no girly shit," I warn them. All the females smile back at me, but Lindsey's smile is sinister. She leans in close, knowing Karma's watching and listening. "Ready to carry my bags? Just so you know, I plan on doing *a lot* of shopping."

"If you need help trying on some of those lacy things, I'm your man, sugar tits."

Karma slams his fist down on the table next to her. "Keep it up, asshole."

"Trust me, I plan on it." I turn my attention back to Lindsey, while Karma fumes behind her. "Now, about those lacy things I mentioned…"

Chapter 4

CORA

SQUEALING, Harrison presses his hands against his ears to dull the deafening sound of passing motorcycles. His brown eyes are wide with glee as they pass, unsure of which one to look at first.

"Look, Momma!" he screeches. "A blue one!"

Since the day my boy was born into this world, he's had an obsession with motorcycles. Why couldn't he like Tonka trucks, or trains, or ponies? Why does it *have* to be motorcycles?

"I see." I smile, loving the way his eyes light up when he's excited. "Come on, buddy, we gotta get home. Momma has to work tonight."

Reluctantly, Harrison reaches out and places his tiny hand in mine, his eyes glued to the road as we walk. It's just after three o'clock in the afternoon, and the streets are filled with tourists and bikers. Parked motorcycles line the sidewalks, all of them positioned at an angle, their finishes glistening in the sun.

"Momma!" he cries again. "That one has a bird on it, like the one on your arm."

I follow the direction of his finger. A black Harley sits on the other side of the road, surrounded by other black Harleys. But the paint job on the one he's talking about makes it stand out. A brightly colored phoenix, its flaming wings spread wide, spans the side of the fuel tank. Its tail curls down and around, the fiery plume of feathers ending near the tail pipe. It's breathtaking.

It's nearly identical to the one I have tattooed on my upper arm.

"Can we go see?" Harrison asks, pulling on my hand, trying his best to drag me to it.

I don't budge. "Sorry, baby, but we have to get home. Nana's waiting for you, and when I left, she was making cookies."

But Harrison is on a mission that not even the promise of fresh-baked cookies can snap him out of. "Please," he whines, his pulling turning to yanking. "I want to see."

"Harrison," I say, keeping my voice firm. Dropping down to his level, I place my hands on his shoulders, turning him until we're eye to eye. "We need to go. I know you love motorcycles, and that phoenix one is very cool, but Momma has to work, and we need to get home.

Maybe tomorrow afternoon we can take a walk down here so you can get a better look at them all, okay?"

His little face is set in an angry scowl, but after a moment, he nods his head and glances back at the phoenix motorcycle with longing.

A biker steps out of the store just behind it, his hands filled with shopping bags, and several women filing out behind him. My heart skitters in my chest when I see TK from the Moose Knuckle Tavern.

He's just as good looking in the daylight as he was under the florescent lights of the bar. And judging by the harem behind him, he knows how to use that to his advantage.

TK looks annoyed as he turns to face them. I don't know what he says, but the girls just laugh and walk on by him, the last one pausing only long enough to pat him on the shoulder before they all disappear into the next shop.

Dropping his head back, TK stares up at the sky for a moment, then deposits the bags into a van down the road. I watch in wonder as he slams the back door shut and places his hands on his hips.

Seriously, why does he have to be so hot? I swore off bikers years ago, for good reason, and this is the first time any of them have ever piqued my interest.

"Momma, come on." Harrison yanks on my hand

again, but this time, in the direction we had been heading.

With a quick shake of my head, I tear my eyes away from TK's rather perfect ass and resume walking toward home. *God, Cora, you need to get laid.*

The walk to our house is a short one, and inside, as promised, my mother is in the kitchen, pulling out a second sheet of freshly baked chocolate chip cookies.

"Hi, Nana," Harrison sings, climbing up onto the stool and reaching for a cookie on the cooling rack.

"Hello, sweet boy. How was summer camp today?"

"Good," he mumbles around a mouthful of gooey goodness.

My mother smiles down at him, then turns her attention to me. "You're gonna be late."

Shit. "Right. Thank you." I press a kiss to the top of Harrison's head, and then one on my mom's cheek. "His teacher said he had a good day, but he looks tired."

"I'm not tired."

"I'm working till close tonight, because it's just me and Stella behind the bar. That is, if she even bothers to show up."

Mom wraps her arms around me, giving me a tight hug. "He'll be fine. Go, make some money, and be safe."

"Bye, baby." In response, he just waves and reaches for another cookie.

"No way, little man." My mother is already turning to deal with him, leaving me to make my escape.

I chuckle when I hear him draw out a long, desperate, "Pleeeeeease," just as I'm walking out the door.

Thank God for my parents. I don't know what I would do without them.

When I'd first found out I was pregnant with Harrison, I had never been more terrified. I was twenty-two, still living at home, and had no support from the baby daddy. Hell, I wouldn't even have known how to get ahold of him if I'd wanted to.

I'd been so ashamed of myself, and was convinced my father would toss me out on my ass, but he hadn't. He became my biggest champion, right alongside my mother.

Because of them and their love for us, Harrison will never know the unnecessary shame I had felt. And it had been unnecessary, because before him, I'd been adrift, floating from party to party, dead-end job to dead-end job, with no discernable future in sight.

Harrison had given me purpose. He'd given me a reason to get up every morning and put an effort into life. He'd given me lessons in selflessness and putting your child's wants and needs first, no matter how hard that was sometimes.

Most of all, he'd brought me closer to my parents.

Mom and Dad had always been good to me, but for

the majority of my youth, I never acknowledged that. I'd taken them and their love for granted. I'd seen the way my mother waited up for me when I went out, and it had pissed me off, because I thought she was being nosy and intrusive. Now, I know she was doing it because she loved me, and would never have been able to fall asleep until she knew I was safe.

I used to roll my eyes at the way my father would wake me up early, every Saturday morning, to go to the dump. I would wonder why the hell he couldn't go himself, and why it had to be so damn early?

He did it because that was our time. The dump was never busy in the mornings, and on many occasions, that was the best time to get a glimpse of the black bears that came to forage through the waste. I'd always loved watching them, just like Harrison loves watching them now. But when we take Harrison, it's not the bears my father and I watch, it's Harrison. His excitement and curiosity fill my heart with more love than I've ever felt, just like my father had with me when I was a child.

A motorcycle revs as it passes, ripping me from my thoughts and reminding me of my surroundings. The Moose Knuckle Tavern is up ahead, and even though it's not yet four o'clock, the parking lot and street around it are already filled with bikes.

People in leather stand around outside, talking,

smoking, and laughing, enjoying the beautiful weather and loud music floating out from inside.

Fucking bike week.

I stop at the edge of the parking lot and take a deep breath. *You can do this, Cora. Go in, make drinks, earn some tips. And if need be, bust some heads.*

My pep talk doesn't quite do the trick, though, because as soon as I get inside, all I want to do is turn around and run right back out.

The bar is packed. Women are dancing around, pressing their bodies against the men who don't seem to mind a bit. But that's not what bothers me. It's the vibe, the aura. Something's off. Something's gonna happen—I can feel it.

Chapter 5

TWATKNOT

THE BOOMING MUSIC at the Moose Knuckle encompasses the entire space, and I can barely hear the woman next to me speak.

"Why do they call you TwatKnot?" The pretty little brunette nestled up under my arm smiles up at me under her thick eyelashes. Her friends look shocked at her question. One of them even nudges her in the ribs with her elbow. "What? I'm just curious."

Which one of my fucking brothers told her my nickname? I'd told her to call me TK, and never elaborated on the extent of what it meant. There was no reason for it, since she'll be a distant memory come morning. *If* she even makes it that far.

I glare over at a few of my brothers. With a shit-eating grin, V flips me the bird. *Fucker.* Part of me wishes I had gone out to one of the other bars that the rest of the club had ventured off to after our group dinner. I just had the unfortunate pleasure of V, Priest, and Burnt tagging along with me. And with all of us, the cut bunnies came to us in droves. Not that I minded.

V laughs. "Yeah, what does it mean?"

"It means I'm gonna kick your lily-white ass later," I growl back at him.

"Love to see you try."

Turning my attention back to the girl, I grin at her. "Ignore whatever these assholes say. And to your question, how about you come back with me to my place tonight and I'll show you?" Her cheeks flush at the proposition.

"And keep us awake all fucking night again," a brother mutters under his breath. I clearly hear him, but she's so focused on me, she probably wouldn't hear a bomb drop.

"What's in it for me?" she coos. The sweet smell of the fruity cocktail she'd brought with her to my table lingers on her breath as she leans over and tries to kiss me. Just inches from my lips, I stop her by placing my finger between us.

"If you have to ask that question, sugar, you may not be able to handle a guy like me," I whisper.

Her breath hitches, pushing her massive tits toward my face. Something I'd planned on doing later if my other plans fell through—without the bra straining to hold them together, and in a much less public setting. Though, that hasn't stopped me before.

"I can handle you."

"Doubt that, but I'd love to see you try." She tries to push against my finger, but I hold my ground. Kissing is too intimate for my tastes. It implies too much for a one-night stand and gives them hope that I'll see them again. I already know she wants more than I'm willing to offer, so it's time to nip that shit in the bud. "Your friends can come too." The statement hits her hard. It has to be to get my point across.

"What?" She leans back, the statement hitting her hard. The color drains from her face and her body goes rigid.

"I'm just messing with you, sugar," I say, trying quickly to recover. She looks nervously at her friends who shrug with indifference, but one of the girls looks over at me curiously, so I shoot her a wink. She bites her lip ring in response, toying with it between her luscious lips. If I go down in burning flames with my true purpose of coming here, she's at least game.

Leaning forward, I grab my beer and finish it in one long swig before setting the bottle down with a thud.

"You ladies need another drink?"

The brunette says nothing, but her friends fire off a list of fruity cocktails and shots. Shoving away from the table, I make my way through the rowdy crowd toward the bar and discover the mouthy bartender I'd offended a few nights ago by ordering a Skinny Bitch.

She's slinging drinks like a pro, smiling at the patrons lining the bar, waving their money at her. An older man to her left reaches out, grabbing her arm, and she immediately recoils. The glare on her face has me ready to step in and handle the situation, but she reacts by forcefully removing his hand in one swift move.

"Touch me again, I'll cut your balls off and nail them to the bar." The way her eyes bore into his, so angry, so determined, makes me straighten my posture, even knowing I'm not on the receiving end of that look. Her threat is clear as day, and I have no doubt she means every fucking word of it.

The man looks shocked at her response. Fingering a couple of twenties from his wallet, he slides them across the wooden bar top. "Didn't mean any harm, ma'am."

"Just keep your hands to yourself." She turns her back to him, and when he leaves, I take his seat. Her dark hair is swept up into a ponytail, with soft waves coiling at the end, flipping around like a fucking bull-whip after dismissing the dickhead who offended her tonight. *At least it wasn't me this time.*

I get lost in the situation I'd just witnessed that I don't notice when she turns her attention to me. A deep grimace crosses her face.

"You lost? Your harem's over there." She points with

a beer bottle to the group of women I'd just left. "Unless you're ordering a drink, you can go right back over there." How'd she know I was here, let alone where I'd been sitting? *She's been watching me.* Intriguing.

"Are you going to bite my head off for ordering a drink tonight, or was that just the first-timer special?" Her eyes widen ever so slightly. I've hit a nerve, just like the other night.

"Only if you try to run your mouth or touch me like that last motherfucker." There's a bite to her words, but I can't put my finger on the reason why. Annoyance, clearly, but there's something else lingering under the surface.

"Wouldn't dream of it. Just here to drink." Having my balls displayed as a trophy on her bar top isn't on the list of things I want to do today.

"Of course you are." She throws her head back and laughs. "So, you want another Skinny Bitch, or would that be skinny bitches?" Her gaze shifts from me to the table behind me.

"Beer's fine. Whatever you have."

Reaching down, she grabs a bottle from the cooler, pops the lid, and slides it over to me. I glance at the label and chuckle. "Jack's Hoppy Ass?"

"You said any beer, and this seemed fitting. Need anything else?"

I rattle off the cocktails the ladies had requested, and

she grimaces at each of them. One by one, she sets the brightly colored drinks down in front of me and rattles off the total. I pull out the cash from my pocket and hand it over, telling her to keep the change.

She goes to help a customer behind me and watches as I bring the bottle to my lips and take a sip. "Not bad. Though, if I'm being honest, it doesn't taste like ass at all."

Her eyes grow wide.

"Something surprising in what I said?"

"No," she replies curtly.

"About the other night... Why did you react that way?"

"What do you mean?" She frowns, trying to cover up her embarrassment. The blush on her cheeks gives her away, though. "Look, I really don't have time for this. I need to get back to work."

"You're going to have to tell me sooner or later. Got another nine days here."

"And there are plenty of bars in Sturgis, so spare us both the trouble and go to a different one."

"Bitch has teeth, man," a guy next to me mutters.

"Go fuck yourself, Hank," she snaps. "One more word out of you, I'll cut you off and send you back to your wife."

Shit, Hank here isn't fucking kidding. This bitch

really does have teeth—sharp, pointed ones. Perfect for tearing up anyone that pisses her off.

"Still waiting for my answer."

She rolls her eyes. "You're going to be waiting a long time."

"Like I said, I have nine days. I can wait you out."

"You don't even know my name."

"That perfectly placed name tag tells me your name, *Cora*." Her face flushes a bright crimson when she looks down and realizes that she is indeed wearing a name tag. But that embarrassment turns to anger in a hot second.

"Wanna know my name?"

"Asshole?"

"Not the first time I've been called that, darlin', but it's TwatKnot. You can call me TK."

"Dream on, TwatKnot." Her snarky words both hit a nerve and turn me on, all at the same time. That's a fucking first.

"Dreaming about me already, Cora? I'm flattered."

"You'd like that, wouldn't you? I don't fuck bikers, man bun."

"That's oddly specific, seeing as you don't even know me. And I don't remember asking you to fuck me, but now that you mention it…"

"Jesus, you're an asshole, all of you. You come in like you own the joint, fuck up and fuck around what you can't shake off, then leave to go home to your women like nothing ever happened. I'm not interested in that bullshit, so you can ride your bike out of my fucking town."

"Ouch." I slam my hand over my heart. "That was harsh." She's feisty, and I'll be damned, I like that.

"I'm sure your harem will kiss your boo boos." She passes a customer's beer over my head and takes his cash. "Now, if you'll excuse me, I'm going to get back to work." She stalks away without so much as a single glance back in my direction.

What the fuck just happened?

CORA

I GRAB the guy's wrist and yank his hand up, jamming it between his shoulder blades and shoving him toward the door.

"Fuckin' bitch," he spits, struggling only slightly out of fear that his arm may snap in two. "Let me go."

"You're done here, Frank. You touch the girls, you're out." The crowd spreads like the red sea as I shove him through.

"You ain't no fuckin' girl, ya fat cunt. Get your hands off me!"

"Hey," somebody snarls, but I don't pay them any mind. I can take care of this asshole myself.

I yank his arm up farther, knowing that if I were to pull it up just a little higher, something would definitely snap. I can feel it. "Should've thought about that before you put your hand on my tit. You're lucky I don't call the police and charge you with sexual assault."

"Fuck you!"

I use his body to push through the main double doors and shove him forward as I release his arm. "Not if you were the last man on the planet. Now go, and don't come back."

Frank's arms whirl and spin, but it's too late. He lands on the front step, his hands coming out just in time to keep his face from smashing off the wood.

I don't wait around to hear what he has to say about that.

Pulling the door closed behind me, I turn, feeling my cheeks flame as the room erupts into cheers, wolf whistles, and laughter.

"You show him, baby."

"Badass bitch right there."

"Wouldn't want to mess with you, honey."

I make my way back to the bar, embarrassed, but laughing as everyone gets in their congratulations. Frank is a local, but he's always causing problems. He's been caught groping girls many times in this bar alone, but this was the first time he'd gained enough liquid courage to dare touch me.

A tall man with the name Priest sewn onto his leather cut leans across the bar and shoves a five-dollar bill into my tip jar. "You don't mess around, do ya, sweetheart?"

I grab him another bottle of Budweiser from the fridge. "Not when assholes like that think they can put their hands where they're not wanted. You can either get eaten alive, or be the bigger predator."

With a grin, Priest tips the bottle toward me. "Respect."

TK comes up behind him and pushes his way forward. He opens his mouth to speak, but I beat him to it. "Another prissy Skinny Bitch for the big bad biker?"

He grins wide. "You're one mean ass woman, you know that? Why do you gotta cut me like that? I'm a payin' customer."

I can't contain my smile as I prepare his odd beverage choice and place it on the bar top in front of him.

Handing me a ten-dollar bill, his face grows serious. "For real, though, that was impressive. Is that something you have to do a lot?"

"This isn't exactly a place frequented by high society. A girl's gotta do what a girl's gotta do."

TK stares at me a moment, and his blue eyes have my belly doing backflips inside of me. God, he's hot. Too hot for his own good and mine.

"I can only imagine the kind of shit you have to deal with in here during the rally," he says, looking around the packed room. "They shouldn't be leaving you to work alone. That shit's not right."

I prepare another order as I ponder his words. "My

boss is usually the one who works this week, but he got into an accident, so now it's just me and a very unreliable new hire."

Just then, Melinda Humphrey sidles up next to TK, flashing him a smile I've seen her use on dozens of men before him. "Hey, handsome. I was over there with my girlfriends, and I was wondering if you could help me with a little bet we've got going."

TK raises his brow, clearly curious, and I snort out a laugh. *Typical.*

Melinda glares at me before continuing. "They bet me that I couldn't get you to give me your number."

Chuckling, TK looks at me, and then at Melinda's table of skanky friends. He waves at the group before turning his attention back to Melinda, giving her a smile that almost melts my panties, and he's not even directing it at me.

God, I wish he'd direct that smile at me.

No, Cora. No, you don't.

"Sure, sweetheart. Got a pen?"

Melinda produces a black permanent marker from her pocket and holds it out to him. Fucking hell. Why can't he see what she's doing?

Plucking the marker from her fingers, he takes off the cap. "So, where do you want it?"

My jaw nearly hits the floor when Melinda leans back and pushes her chest forward. She pulls the front of her shirt down so low, I can see her nipples through her lacy bra.

Grinning, he leans forward and writes out his number, looking like a man on a mission.

Yuck.

So why can't I look away?

I try to keep from glaring as TK writes the number eight, quickly followed by a six, and then a seven across her chest, even going so far as to slip the tip of the marker just inside the edge of her bra, hiding parts of the number in her intimate areas.

Disgust and anger wash over me, but then he glances over and winks at me. I'm in shock when he writes the numbers five, three, zero, nine.

"Thank you," she purrs, taking the marker, her voice full of phony flirtation. "If you're lucky, maybe I'll give you a call sometime."

TK nods. "I hope you do, sweetheart."

Melinda flashes him a smile and heads back to her table. It's not until we watch her reveal her chest to them, and seeing their excitement at their friend's achievement, that TK and I burst into laughter.

"How long do you think it'll take her to figure it out?"

"Long enough for me to get the fuck out of here."

"I'd advise it. Melinda's as close as you can get to a town bicycle around here, and she has the baby daddies to prove it." She and her friends squeal loudly, clinking their drinks together in triumph. "By the looks of it, you have about five more seconds before she comes back over here. You'd better run."

TK looks at me in mock fear. "Have a good night, Cora."

"You too."

I watch with more interest than I should as he walks back to his friends. God help me. The man looks just as good from the back as he does from the front.

Chapter 7

TWATKNOT

HARD ROCK BLASTS through the open field where the makeshift stage sits front and center amongst the sea of leather, beer, and scantily clad women.

V passes a fresh bottle my way. "Another beer, TK?" I've lost count of the number I've consumed since we made it to the music festival this morning. It's been a long time since I've been this hammered, but it feels fucking good.

"Fuck yeah!" a girl next to me screams when they finish their song. "I love you, BSC!" Her small, but perky tits poke out of the thin white tank top, the material soaked through from the beer being sprayed into the crowd.

"What she said," I slur, guzzling the liquid down my throat. It tastes too good for this early in the morning. If I keep this up, by the end of the week, my liver is going to demand an intervention.

"How you feelin', big guy?" Priest asks Karma, who's swaying on his feet. His response is to flip him off.

I laugh. "I'll take it that you feel as good as me."

To be honest, I've never seen him cut loose like he has this week. Although, he verbally assaulted me after getting back from shopping duty with the ladies. I probably deserved it, seeing as I plucked out the little lace number that Lindsey had picked out and attempted to model it for him. But meh, shit happens. So, besides that little hiccup, all my brothers seem relaxed. My idea to get away is doing us all some good. We needed this more than any of us realized, with all the shit that's been thrown our way.

The pretty little groupie leans back and grinds her ass against my cock in time to the music.

"Are you dancing, fuckface?" V laughs. "Dude, you're shit at it."

If he was as drunk as I was, he'd be shit at it too. Ignoring his critiques, I lean into her and let her do her thing until the band's set ends. She spins on her heel, pressing those tiny tits into my chest.

"I'm Candy," she preens.

"I bet you are, sweetness."

"I said no, asshole," a female voice shouts from behind me, drawing my attention away from Candy.

I can barely hear it over the crowd, but something about her tone keys me into the conversation. Something sobering. I search for where it's coming from, but there are so many people. I peer over at Priest, who's listening for it too. Yeah, he heard it. It's not just booze fucking with my head. As we both scan the crowd, I hear it again.

"Get the fuck off me!" I close my eyes, zeroing in on the voice as hard as I can with the amount of alcohol in my system affecting my concentration. As I'm listening, a firm hand clasps my shoulder. I open my eyes to see Priest pointing off to our right.

"Looks like your friend needs saving."

Every cell in my body sobers at the scene several rows back from us. There stands Cora in a heated argument with a fucking giant of a man in front of her. Dude must have a foot and a half on her. Her face is upturned with that defiant fucking sneer that's grown on me over the last few days. Her hands are resting on her hips as she shouts at him, and he reaches out and grabs her arm, yanking her forward. The second he touches her, I take off toward them, with Priest hot on my heels.

I shove through a group blocking my way, ignoring their shit talk as I go. My focus is solely on getting to her and the hand I intend to break and display like a fucking trophy on my bike if it's still on her when I get to them.

Touching a woman after she says no, especially Cora, isn't going to happen on my watch.

Neither of them sees me coming until I am already there, cocked and ready to lay his ass out. Priest tries to cut in front of me, but I throw out my arm, blocking him. "I got this." Seeing the look on my face, Priest nods. Knowing he's got my back, I continue on until I'm only inches away from the big bastard. I force myself between them, forcing him to release her, and pushing Cora behind me.

"I think the lady said no," I drawl.

"This doesn't involve you. If that fucking big bitch—"

My bare knuckles connect with his jaw, sending him flying back. "You done?"

"Fuck you!"

I barely get out a warning to Cora to back up before he barrels headfirst into my stomach. I reel from the impact, but drag up my elbow and land a few shots to the back of his head. The fucker just keeps going, shoving me closer and closer to the crowd behind me. I shift my weight, throwing him off balance, and take my shot. I throw a few uppercuts to his gut that land with a thud. He pushes away from me, clutching his stomach with his arm.

"Holy fuck, man. If she's yours, put a fuckin' patch on her."

I'm ready to rip the motherfucker to shreds for

simply being an asshole, when Priest and a few of the others come and stand next to me.

"Need some help?" Karma inquires, smirking.

Relaxing my stance, I take a step back. "I've got it under control." Eyes still on the wannabe rapist, I jab my finger into his chest. "You so much as sniff in her fucking direction, it'll be your last breath on this earth. Understood?"

I can feel the hate pouring off him in waves, but he bobs his head up and down in agreement. That's not good enough, though. I want him to say it aloud. I want her to hear his words.

"Say it, asshole."

"All right!" he shouts. "I won't touch your fucking woman."

My woman? Cora's hardly my woman, but if that idea keeps her safe from this guy coming around again, he can believe whatever the fuck he wants. Guys like him make me fucking sick. I may be a player, but I would never fucking force a woman into my bed. Not against her will, and sure as fuck not if she says no.

"Allow me to take out the trash." Grabbing the guy by the collar, Priest pulls him closer. Karma and Stone-Face follow behind, the three of them moving the man toward the exit. I wait until they're out of sight before turning to find Cora, who's standing not too far from me, looking livid.

"I had it handled," she snaps, her arms crossed against those big tits of hers, heaving up and down with her rapid breaths. "I didn't need your help."

"A simple thank you would suffice."

"I'm not thanking you. I can take care of myself."

"I know you can." I'd seen it for myself when she hauled that drunk out of the bar the other night. Shit, she'd impressed me with how well she handled herself. "But you shouldn't fucking have to."

She looks away.

"Show me your arm." I step forward, but she takes a step back.

"I'm fine," she says, her voice softer now. After a moment, she uncrosses her arms and shows me where he'd manhandled her. The red imprint of his hand is seared onto her skin. My eyes narrow, but she pulls away and folds her arms over her chest again, like it's a protective instinct. "Seriously, I'm fine. He was just an asshole. It's nothing I haven't dealt with before."

I don't like that one bit, but it helps me understand exactly why she's as tough as she is. Being a Sturgis local, she would have to know how to handle herself around handsy bikers. Bikers that give dudes like me a bad fucking rep.

"Are you here alone?"

"No. My friends are over at the bar, getting another round."

That's bullshit. Friends would've been here to help her. Not a single person around her stepped in to stop him until I did. No, she's here alone.

"I want to believe you, but I think you're lying to me."

"Why would I lie to you?" she argues.

God, she's stubborn. "I'll wait until they come back."

"That's not necessary."

"It is if you don't want something like that happening again."

"Not likely," she snorts. "The guy was clearly drunk, looking for what he thought was an easy lay.

"Nothing is easy about you, darlin'."

"Seriously, TK, I'm fine. Go on back to your buddies." She gazes over my shoulder. "Looks like your fan club is missing you."

I follow her line of sight to Candy and her friend, glaring in our direction.

"They're not important."

I can tell she doesn't like that, but she says nothing more. We stand in silence, with her watching the crowd and me watching her. Normally, her hair is up in a ponytail, but today, it's hanging loose around her shoulders. I have to admit, I like it down. It's very pretty.

"I'm gonna go find them," she insists, looking uncomfortable just standing there.

Knowing there's no point in arguing, I reach my hand out in front of her. "Give me your phone."

"What? Why?" Her nose wrinkles in adorable confusion. Spying it sticking out of her pocket, I just reach out and take it. "Hey! What are you doing? Give that back!"

"I will when I'm done," I tell her, peering down at the lock screen. *Shit.* "Unlock it."

"No."

I drop my head back and sigh. "Are you always this difficult? Just unlock your fucking phone, Cora."

Growling, she snatches it from my hand and slides her finger across the screen before handing it back to me. I find her contacts and punch in my number, leaving her a bit of a surprise when she goes searching later, then hand it back to her.

"I put my number in your contacts. If that fucker shows back up, or if you need me for absolutely anything, you get hold of me right away. Text or call."

"Why would I do that?"

I inch closer to her, just enough that I can hear her sharp intake of breath.

"Because you might be tough, sweetheart, but nobody should be fighting all these battles on their own."

Chapter 8

CORA

I SLIP FAR ENOUGH into the crowd that TK can't see me anymore, but I'm close enough to watch as he rejoins his buddies. A pretty brunette with a pixie cut runs up and wraps her arms around his neck, pressing her tits against him as she sways, trying to get him to dance with her.

Why had he done that? The guy had been an asshole for sure, but I could've gotten away. I'd done it before, and I'm pretty sure that last guy who messed with me had to get a testicle surgically removed.

I don't know why I even came here. Curiosity, maybe? It had been a long time since I'd been home for bike week, and when I'd heard that Rock Townsend was playing tonight, I'd made sure to take this one night off to check it out.

My mother hadn't been too happy when I told her

where I was going, especially when I'd mentioned coming here with Rachel and Nicki, because she'd never liked them. I don't like them much either sometimes, but this town isn't exactly overflowing with possible friendships for me. And even if Rachel and Nicki were world class bitches, at least they were familiar bitches.

"Who was that guy?" Rachel asks, sliding up beside me, her overly made-up eyes trained on TK. Part of me wants to punch the admiration right off her stupid face.

"Just a guy from the bar." I move to walk away, but Rachel and Nicki stay rooted to their spots.

Grinning over at me, Nicki grabs Rachel's hand. "Come on, Cora. Introduce us to your sexy friend."

The two of them giggle and stumble as they make their way toward TK and the other Black Hoods. I knew I shouldn't have come with them. I hadn't hung out with them since before I'd had Harrison, and in this instant, I remember why. The only thing they understand is partying, meaningless sex, and keeping me firmly in my place as the DUFF in our trio, the designated fat, ugly friend.

"Nicki," I call, hurrying after them, desperate to intervene before they get anywhere near him.

My fingers catch the back of Rachel's shirt when we're just a few feet away.

"Where'd your lady friend go, TK?" Priest inquires loudly over the music, but I'm close enough to hear him. I know he's talking about me.

TK responds, and I hear his voice loud and clear.

"There's lots of free pussy around here, man. You think I'm gonna go chasin' after a fat, mouthy bartender that would probably bite my dick off if I even tried to get near her?"

His words hit me like a punch to the gut, and I freeze. Rachel heard him as well, because she claps a hand over her mouth and shouts giddily, "Oh my God, that's hilarious!"

My heart squeezes in my chest, and the pain in my belly grows, as if his words were splitting me wide open.

Rachel's high-pitched squeal gets Priest's attention, and his surprised eyes soften as they meet mine. I watch his lips move, but I can't hear his whispered words. And then, in slow motion, TK turns and sees me standing just behind him.

"Oh, fuck," a buddy of his mutters, causing Nicki to giggle along with Rachel.

I know the instant our eyes meet that he knows I heard him. His face blanches under the strings of lights, and his mouth drops open.

Without a word, I run.

I run from TK, calling my name, and Rachel and Nicki's howling laughter, toward the exit.

Why did I ever agree to come here with those bitches? They'd never done anything but make a fool out of me at every turn, so why did I think after a few years had passed, they'd changed?

And TK... Why did his words hurt so bad? It's not like I haven't been called worse. Some of the drunks at the bar have gotten pretty creative with their insults when I cut them off from their alcohol, or break up a fight they're itching to get into.

But those guys were always drunk. And though their insults were shitty, they were said in anger, in the heat of the moment. They weren't personal. Yet TK had said them because he meant them. He may have been nice to me these past few days, even helping me out with that handsy prick a few minutes ago, but it's clear he doesn't see me in any sort of positive light.

Fat, mouthy bartender.

Those three words cut me to the quick. And to think, I almost saw him as a friend.

I push my way out of the building and onto the street, needing to get as far away as possible from TK's words, and Rachel and Nicki's cruel laughter.

My fingernails bite into the palms of my hands as I turn the corner and rush down the street. I grew up in this town. I know every shortcut and hiding place there is, and I use that knowledge to my advantage.

It's not until I'm a few blocks away, walking through the Center Street Park, that I slow down. My chest heaves, desperate for oxygen. Getting my breathing under control, I head toward the empty swings and choose the one on the end to drop down into.

Fat, mouthy bartender.

Fuck him. Fuck TK and his stupid hair, and his big, stupid muscles, and those stupid blue eyes. Fuck him for making me feel this way.

The truth is, I know I'm on the bigger side. I'm curvy. I know I'm not exactly society's ideal specimen of a woman, but I look damn good, and I know it. I'm no skinny bitch like Rachel, and I don't walk around wearing corsets in public like Nicki, but I'm not ashamed of my body.

Shoving off with the tips of my toes, swing. I swing so high, the poles threaten to come up out of the ground. I swing until I can breathe properly again. I breathe until I decide I don't want to go back to that concert just so I can shove my foot up TK's ass.

I'm not the least bit ashamed of me. The only thing I'm ashamed of is that TK is a biker, and I know better than to think any biker is a decent guy, because he's not. He's a shallow, callous asshole, and I won't be making that same mistake twice.

TWATKNOT

FAT, *mouthy bartender that would probably bite my dick off if I even tried to get near her.*

I'm such a fucking asshole. No, I'm lower than that. I'm worse than the guy who laid a hand on her at the concert. At least he was just some drunken stranger looking to get laid. She knew me. I came to her rescue, then put her down the second one of my brothers teased me about her. And when I saw her standing there... Fuck, I'll never forget the way she looked at me.

The way the color drained from her face.

The tear that snuck out and ran down her cheek before she could wipe it away.

She unknowingly haunts me with that look I've committed to memory in the hours since it happened.

"Goddammit." Why didn't I go after her when I had the chance? I just let her leave without even trying to explain. I could blame it on being drunk, but the only person to blame is me and my stupid fucking ego.

"The fuck was that, TK?" Judge inquires with an arched brow.

"Just handling a situation," I mutter.

"That why the bartender from the other night ran out of here like a bat out of hell?"

Fuck. He'd seen what had happened, and likely heard what I said too. Fucking great.

"She didn't want my help." I shrug. "I gave it anyway."

"I can see how well that worked out for you. You good?"

"I'm fine," I lie. I'm far fucking from it, but getting Judge involved is not an option. The last thing I need right now is to have one of his fatherly you're-fucking-shit-up discussions in the middle of this godforsaken field over my love life. I'd been witness to enough of those lately to know the script he'd use by heart. "I'll deal with it."

He gives me a once-over before turning his attention back to Grace, who's singing along to the music at his side, leaving me to stew all on my own.

Why did I care so much about hurting her? What is it about her that's making me feel so guilty? I'm sure I've hurt dozens of women with the shit that comes out of my mouth, but with Cora, it just feels different. So fucking different. That beautiful, confident, cocky woman that dishes my shit back at me like a seasoned pro. She's been through some shit, that's apparent enough, but she's still her own person. I like that about her, but I've gone and fucked that up.

Women have always come easy to me. Well, the sex part, at least. But friendships? I have no idea where to even begin with that kind of relationship. The closest thing I've ever come to a female friend is with Lindsey, and she's more like a sister to me than a friend. *Lindsey.* She'd know what to do.

I barely let the idea get through my head before I see her standing next to Karma with a beer in her hand. Trudging up to the crowd, she spots me immediately.

"Come to lick your wounds, TK?" Karma teases.

"Something like that. I need to borrow your girl." Karma tenses up, eyeing me up and down like a fucking threat.

"Whoa, there." I raise my hands in surrender. "Not for that shit, man. I'm not that fucking stupid. I just need to talk to her." Territorial fucking assholes, all of us. A sober Karma would know better than to suspect that I wanted to do anything more than to talk to her, but the drunk version standing in front of me isn't so keen on the idea.

"It's okay." Patting his chest, Lindsey plants a kiss on his lips. "You know I can kick his ass."

"Doubtful, sweetheart," I snort. "But seriously, K, I just need to talk to her. I need some advice, so I could use some of that brain shit she does."

Lindsey eyes me warily, doing that assessing shit she's good at. "We'll be right back."

Begrudgingly, he fucking releases her.

"You stay where I can see you," he warns. Lindsey smiles at him before moving toward me. Grabbing my arm, she leads me over to the edge of the area we were congregating together. The music is still loud, but low enough that we can still hear each other.

Crossing her arms over her chest, she faces me, narrowing her eyes. "All right, what did you do now?"

"There's this girl."

"Tell me something I don't know, TK. It's always about a girl." Her eyes suddenly widen. "Please don't tell me you fucked some chapter president's old lady and he's hunting your ass down, because that's a problem for my uncle, not me. I can't talk your way out of that."

"No," I rasp. Is this how my club sees me? A manwhore without a conscience? Jesus, how stupid do they think I am? "It's not like that."

"Then what's it like? Because you coming to me first is weird. I'm not some patron saint of fuckboys."

"Jesus, just let me tell you." I start from the beginning, from the first time I saw Cora at the bar, and finally end with what had recently transpired. Lindsey listens to me rattle on like one of her patients, taking in the full story with keen interest.

"And she heard what you said? You're sure of it?"

"If you'd seen her face, you wouldn't be asking me that." The image of it lingers clear as day in my mind.

She's quiet for a moment, looking thoughtful. When I think she's about to give me some meaningful words of wisdom shit, she throws her head back and laughs. "Jesus, TK. You're so fucked."

"That's not helping, Lindsey," I snarl, my jaw tight. "I need to know what to do to fix this."

"I'm sorry," she says, continuing to laugh. "It's just that I've never seen you this hung up about a girl before. That's not at all your MO."

I scrub my hands over my face in frustration. Maybe coming to her was a mistake after all. Her absolute joy at my embarrassing predicament is not what I came to her for. I came for advice, and all she's doing is ridiculing me.

"Okay," she barely gets out through her howling laughter. When it finally dies down, she takes a deep breath, settling herself. "If you were one of my clients, I'd probably advise you to reflect inward about why you said something so disgusting before talking to her. But I know you. You think going in there headfirst is going to fix it. It's not. If you're right that she has some baggage, you've re-opened a wound for her."

"So what do I do? I'm asking honestly here, Lindsey. This is all new to me."

"That depends. We've only got a few more days here. If she doesn't mean anything to you, just walk away. That's the simplest course of action."

"And if I don't want to do that?"

"Then you're fucked, plain and simple. Rebuilding trust is going to take time, and calling her what you did —which was a fucking dick move, by the way, and I should kick your ass for that—is not just going to magically go away by saying sorry. Women don't forgive easily. Look at how long it took me to forgive myself for all the things I did, for things that Karma did. It took years, and you have days at best."

Days to do what Lindsey said could take years. She's right, I am fucked. Maybe walking away would be the easiest thing to do for me, but for Cora? What I said could change a lot for her and affect her more than I care to admit.

"What would you do?"

"If you like her, fix it. That's the only way you're going to be able to live with the pain you've caused her."

"Thanks," I tell her, meaning it.

"For what? It's kind of my job."

Not true. Lindsey and Blair may have gone to school to help others work through their mental health issues, but they're so much more than their education to this club, to their men, and to me. I feel ashamed for not realizing it until now.

"For being you." I squeeze her shoulder. "You better get back to your man. He's eyeing me up and down again."

She sees him doing just that and sighs. "You're good, right?"

"I will be, thanks to you."

She looks me over before turning on her heel and heading back to our group, leaving me to make my decision.

The only way I'm going to figure this shit out is to talk to her, to apologize, and hope she accepts it. That's all I have. The only problem is that the bar doesn't open for hours, and I have no idea if she's even working today. I'm kicking myself for not getting her number when I put mine in her phone. It would've made this so much easier than just showing up and pissing her off even more, but the only option I have is to sit and wait for the bar to open.

Chapter 10

CORA

CLIMBING OUT OF THE SHOWER, I send a wish out into the universe for the night off, but I know it's useless. Besides, when was the last time I got my way?

Why do you even care, Cora? He's just another asshole biker that'll be gone in a few days. What's the big deal?

But that's the big question, isn't it? TK was nothing to me in the grand scheme of things, so why did his words make me want to put on my baggiest sweater and comfiest jogging pants to wear to work tonight? Something that would cover my body, shielding it from the judgmental eyes of everyone that comes into the Moose Knuckle.

But jogging pants aren't exactly bartender attire. And besides… fuck TK.

Forty-five minutes later, my hair hangs down my back in soft, loose curls. My make-up is done, and I'd even pulled out that new contouring palette I'd bought months ago and never used.

I slide on my ripped, high-rise jeans, the ones that make my ass look like a round, juicy apple. And when I pull out the bright red halter top, I realize I've done this on purpose.

I know TK is going to be there tonight, and I know that son of a bitch is going to come up with some bullshit excuse about why he said what he did, and try to cram some pitiful apology down my throat. But I'm not having it. I'm going to look hot as fuck while he tries, though.

I walk into the living room and plant a kiss on the top of my son's head.

"Wow, Momma. You look pretty."

"Thank you, baby."

My father eyes me from the couch. "You do look pretty. Who's the guy?"

"Oh, Dad. You know you're the only man for me."

"Hey!" Harrison cries, a frown creasing the smooth skin between his eyebrows. "What about me?"

"You're the only man for me too," I assure him.

"You can't have two mans."

My father sits back and crosses his ankle over his knee before taking a sip of his beer. "You'd be surprised, champ. Girls as pretty as your momma can have as many mans as they want."

"Dad!" I gasp, picking up a decorative pillow and chucking it at him.

He laughs, catching it midair, then stuffs it behind his head, as if he'd been hoping I'd throw it all along. He and Harrison go back to watching the ball game on TV, and I make my way into the kitchen to grab my purse.

"Who's the guy?" my mom asks, stepping out of the pantry, scaring the shit out of me.

"God, Mom, don't do that," I wheeze out, clutching my hand to my chest. "And what do you mean, 'who's the guy'?"

Placing a can of peaches on the counter, she gives me a knowing look. "You put more effort into your appearance than you usually do. And that top shows a lot more of your ladies than we usually see."

My cheeks heat as I look down at the very prominent line of cleavage I'm sporting. With a heavy sigh, I plop down onto the stool across from her and place my forehead on the cool countertop. "It's not a guy. Well, I mean, not really." I raise my head and look at her. "I heard someone say something about my weight last night, and I keep telling myself it doesn't matter, but I guess it does. I just want to show him that I may be a little bigger than some, but I'm still a desirable woman."

My mother frowns. "Desirable? Cora, you're beautiful."

I snort. "All mothers think their kids are beautiful."

"Yes, that's true, but it's different in this case. Honey, look in a damn mirror. You're not some rail thin, over-done Barbie doll like that Rachel girl you still talk to. You're soft and feminine. You have big, beautiful brown eyes, and your skin is like silk." Reaching out, she grabs my hands and squeezes them in hers. "Why do you care what this guy says, anyway? You never usually pay any mind to that stuff."

"I have no idea, Momma. It just feels different this time, more personal somehow."

Releasing my hands, she cups my face. "Personal or not, if this guy made you feel poorly about yourself for even a fraction of a second, he's not worth the time or effort you put into your appearance today. Forget him, Cora." Her lips turn up in a wicked grin. "But since you're looking like a million bucks tonight, you go to work, and you make that asshole see just what he's missing out on."

Chapter 11

TWATKNOT

I'VE BEEN SITTING in the parking lot outside the Moose Knuckle all day under the sweltering sun, watching for her to pull up. As soon as the open sign clicks on, and the early crowd starts funneling into the bar for karaoke night, I waste zero time and head inside, making a beeline straight to the bar, but my heart sinks to the floor when I see a man setting up the glasses, and Cora nowhere in sight.

"Cora here?" I ask the guy.

"She's in the back." Drying a glass, he rests his hip against the waist-high beer cooler and studies me. "Are you a friend or something?"

"Or something," I mutter. Before I'd opened my big mouth, I would've been happy to answer that question with a yes.

"Want a beer while you wait?"

Fuck yeah, I'll take anything to calm my racing heart. But then again, beer is what got me into this mess in the first place. Deciding it's the last thing I need right now, I decline and pretend not to notice when the guy continues to eye me with suspicion before moving on down the bar to take orders.

With nothing else to do, I take a seat on the barstool and I wait, and wait. I wait long enough that I'm starting to think this asshole lied to me about her being here at all. But as soon as karaoke starts up, she finally appears.

Her eyes are dull, like the light behind them has dimmed. Her cocky smile has been replaced with a deep-set frown. Guilt punches me in the gut, because I'm fairly certain I'm the reason she looks like this.

But the rest of her... Fuck, the rest of her looks incredible with those soft curves and ample cleavage. Her silky hair shines in the fluorescent lights, making her look like a damn angel from above. I'd always found Cora to be attractive, but I'd never really *looked* at her before right now.

She's much more than attractive, she's ethereal.

I watch her take orders at the opposite end of the bar, marveling at the poise and confidence she has when dealing with a rowdy group. The woman is fearless.

A friendly smile adorns her lips as she shoots the shit with the customers, but the instant her eyes land on me, her smile damn near shatters.

"Cora, I'm—"

"Get the fuck out of my bar," she orders, pointing to the doors.

"Cora, please," I try again, but she's ignoring me now. When she takes the drink order from the guy sitting to my left, she gives him a wide smile while pretending I'm not even there.

Goddammit.

"Cora." This time, her name comes out as more of a command, and the people sitting around lower their voices, wondering what the hell's going on.

"Get out," she repeats, not once looking at me.

"Not until we talk."

"I have zero interest in talking to you."

"Come on, Cora," I plead, my voice sounding more like a whine at this point. "I waited in the fucking parking lot all day to talk to you."

Snagging a glass from the bar, she rolls her eyes.

I rake my hand over my face and growl. Is it always this hard to apologize to a woman? If it is, then it's no damn wonder men surrender the second they fuck up.

"Why are you acting like this? I'm trying to apologize to you."

She halts mid-stride and pivots, glaring coldly at me. "Oh, I'm sorry. Are you used to bimbos who fall at your feet whenever you grace them with your presence?"

I frown, taken aback. "What the fuck are you talking

about?" Why won't she give me a chance to explain? She's mad, furious, even, and I get it, but I came here to try to make amends. I just need her to listen to me.

"I'm just a fat, mouthy bartender, remember? I don't exactly fit into the mold of whores and porn stars that you normally slum around with." Her words hit me like an arrow to the chest. I deserve that. Hell, I more than deserve that. "Now, if you'll fucking leave," she continues, "I have a job to do."

More people crowd around me, none of them bothering to hide their interest in our back and forth. *Great, a fucking audience.*

"I'm not leaving until you give me a chance to explain," I tell her sternly, working hard to keep my voice even.

"Either you get out of my bar, or I'll fucking throw you out myself. Choice is yours."

She stalks off, her nose in the air, with her sweet ass swaying from side to side. Tapping the other bartender on the shoulder, he looks over at me as she whispers something in his ear. With a nod, they switch places, with him taking over my end of the bar.

I drop my head forward and sigh. I'm getting nowhere fucking fast if she won't even talk to me.

The old man next to me chuckles. "First time apologizing?"

"That obvious?"

"Pretty sure the whole bar knows. You're shit at it, by the way."

"Uh, thanks?"

"Want some advice?" Lifting his wrinkled hand, he points over at Cora. "A female that mad? You need more than words, buddy. You need a grand gesture."

I give him a blank stare. "A what?"

"Grand gesture."

"What the fuck is that?"

"You really are new at this, aren't you?" He swivels around on his stool and shakes his head. "How do you normally get a woman to talk to you?"

"I don't," I admit. "They seek me out."

This makes him laugh. "And that's your problem right there—women chase you. You never learned to chase them."

"You said you were gonna give me advice, old man, but all I'm hearing is you laughing at me, giving me no fucking direction on what to do in this situation."

He tips his head, acknowledging my words. "I apologize. Been a long time since a young buck like yourself needed advice on how to deal with a woman from an old ass like me, but I mean it when I say you need a grand gesture. Look around you. There's a whole lotta ways you can grab her attention in a crowd like this. Get yourself an audience, and she'll have no choice but to talk to you." Grabbing his beer from the bar top, he slides off the stool and walks away, calling back, "Good luck."

I continue to stew, wishing I'd taken that beer when the DJ announces the next person up to sing, and that's when it hits me. Like a man on a mission, I stride over to the DJ booth.

"How do I do this shit?" I ask him.

"The sign-up list is right there."

I peer over at the paper in front of his station and see every fucking spot is full. This won't do. Reaching into my wallet, I finger out a hundred-dollar bill and hand it to him.

"That's yours if you let me go next, and I'll give you another hundred if this works."

Grinning, the DJ plucks the bill from my fingers. "What song?"

"The fuck if I know. One that'll make a woman stop being pissed at me."

He gives me a knowing nod. "An 'I fucked up' track. I got you, man. What's your name?"

"TK," I mutter.

He goes back to his setup and punches some buttons. The woman on the stage screeches out some pop song, grinding her hips like a geriatric Britney Spears. As horrible as she is, the crowd goes wild once she's finished.

Am I really gonna fucking do this?

I eye the crowd, thankful that none of my brothers are here to see me do this. I can't sing for shit, and I'm about to make a total fool out of myself. But if it makes Cora stop and listen to me, even for a few minutes, it'll be worth it.

The DJ leans around the barrier. "All right, TK. You're up."

My feet feel like they're encased in blocks of cement as I step up onto the stage. Bright lights beam down from the ceiling, almost blinding the fuck out of me. As soon as I step up to the mic, someone in the crowd yells out something I can't quite hear.

"Up next," the DJ announces, "we have TK with "If I Can Turn Back Time" by Cher."

Did that motherfucker say Cher?

"Dude, what the fuck?" I call out from behind the mic.

He just smiles and points to the screen where words start to scroll as the music cues up. When my eyes adjust to the bright lights, I can see Cora resting against the bar, arms crossed, staring a hole right through me.

Here goes nothin', old man. Your grand gesture shit better work, because I'm about to embarrass the shit out of myself.

My mouth opens, and Cher's apology song spills from my lips. Well, most of it does, anyway. I try like hell to follow along with the words, but they're flying off the screen so fast, I miss most of them. Focusing on that, and trying to see if Cora's watching me, becomes difficult.

"Fuck it," I mutter to myself. This grand gesture is about to turn up to eleven. *This is for you, Cora.* Grabbing the mic from the stand, I belt out the words like I'm fucking Cher herself. I gyrate as I sing, my arms open as I add as much theatrics to my performance as possible.

The women in the audience hoot and holler with every swish of my hips, none of them caring that I'm single-handedly butchering the song. I finally get to the end, my heart pounding, and the room goes wild.

Grinning from ear to ear, I take a bow. As I'm bent forward, receiving my hard-earned accolades, I look toward the bar just in time to see Cora walking out the front door.

Chapter 12

CORA

"OH, WOW!" Harrison cries, running toward a motorcycle with a sidecar painted to look like Scooby Doo's Mystery Machine.

"You like Scooby Doo, little man?" the guy sitting in it asks.

Harrison scrunches up his nose. "What's a Scooby Doo?"

The guy barks out a laugh that sounds like he'd just finished smoking seventeen packs of cigarettes in a row. When he settles down, he looks at me and grins. "Scoob's not a thing anymore?"

I shrug. "I like him."

Harrison sees another motorcycle he likes and starts after it. "Harrison, slow down," I call out. "Wait for me." Nodding to the man, I take off after my son. For someone with such short little legs, he sure can move. "Harrison!"

A large man, wearing faded jeans and a leather cut, steps out of nowhere and scoops Harrison up into his massive arms. The instant my eyes meet his, every drop of blood I possess drains from my body.

"Put my son down."

Big Dick, the president of the Screwballs MC, stares down at the little boy in his arms. "You're a handsome little fucker, aren't ya?"

Harrison's eyes grow wide. "You said a bad word."

Big Dick throws his head back and laughs, then turns his attention to me. "Long time no see, Cora. Rachel told me about the boy, but I didn't believe it. He's got my eyes, doesn't he?"

I inhale slowly, willing my racing heart to calm and my voice to remain even. "Put my son down."

Harrison's face changes from curious to worried. "Momma?"

"It's okay, baby."

Big Dick chuckles. "Your momma ever tell you about your daddy, son?"

"I don't have a daddy."

"You don't?" Big Dick feigns surprise. "How'd you get here if you don't have a daddy?"

"We walked."

Big Dick laughs again, and the sound snaps me out of my sudden paralysis. Stepping forward, I take advantage of his distraction and pluck Harrison out of his arms.

Without a word, I turn and hurry down the road, but I hear his heavy boots on the pavement just behind me. "You ever plannin' on tellin' me I got a son, Cora?"

My car. I just need to get to my car.

"I got a right to know my boy, Cora. He has a right to know his daddy."

Harrison clasps my shirt in his little fist, looking scared to death. "Momma?"

"It's okay, baby. Just look at Momma, okay? Just look at Momma."

My car comes into view up ahead, but should I even stop there? Big Dick is right behind me, and as soon as I stop, he'll stop too. He'll know what car I drive, and he'll be able to grab me.

The place is crowded, bikers everywhere, but I've never felt so alone. None of these people would stick their necks out to help me, especially if it meant going against the president of the Screwballs MC.

I have no choice.

I hit the unlock button on the key in my pocket and run around to the driver's side. Opening the back door, I place Harrison on the seat. "Get into your booster, baby, and buckle up."

I take in Harrison's wide eyes and I shut the door. He's never put himself in his seat. I don't think he even knows how to buckle up, but I can't afford to stop. I need to—

A large hand wraps around my arm, and before I know it, I'm pressed against the back door of my car. "Slow the fuck down and talk to me, Cora. You owe me that much."

If I had the ability to shoot fire, I swear this is the time I would do it. His words spark more anger than I've ever felt, and flames erupt inside of me. "I don't owe you shit, asshole. Now let me go."

"That's my son."

I look him straight in the eyes, praying he doesn't see through my lie when I grit out the words, "He's not."

Big Dick smirks, but there's no humor in it. His eyes are black and cold. Emotionless. His fingertips bite into my upper arms as he pulls me close, bringing us nose-to-nose. "That is my son."

"He's NOT!" I roar, slamming my knee between his legs.

Hitting my target, Big Dick's fingers disappear from my arms. Seeing him bent over at the waist, I shove him back and slip into the driver's seat, jamming the lock button the instant the door closes.

"You bitch!" he hollers, slamming his fist against my window. "You're fucking dead, bitch!"

"Momma?" Harrison whimpers. "Momma, why is that man so angry?"

Without answering, I turn the key in the ignition. "Just buckle up, baby."

I pull out of my parking space, watching through the rearview mirror as Big Dick runs back toward the main road, likely to his motorcycle, his frame bent slightly as he struggles to move through the pain.

Fuck.

"Momma, who was that bad man?"

I continue down the road at a snail's pace, resisting the urge to blare the horn at all the pedestrians littering the streets. "Don't you worry about that, baby. Momma's got you."

A small parade of motorcycles passes by, and I wait, desperate to make a right-hand turn, but unable to move. Suddenly, in the rearview, I see him.

His motorcycle's low to the ground, with long ape hanger handlebars and a giant confederate flag hanging off the backend, and he's getting closer by the second.

Shit, shit, shit!

What the fuck do I do now? If I go home, he'll know where I live, if Rachel hasn't already told him.

Rachel. That bitch and I are going to be having words. I may just kill her.

With no other ideas, I press the number on my dashboard to call my father. The phone rings and rings, and then finally, his voicemail up.

"Ugh," I groan, stabbing the button to disconnect the call.

What do I do? What do I do?

Big Dick is closer now. In another few seconds, he'll be close enough to touch the back bumper of my car.

"Momma, he's coming."

"I know. It's okay."

It's not okay. Fucking hell, it's not okay.

I try my father again, racking my brain, desperate to think of who else to call.

The police? I could call them, but because it's bike week, they'll take forever. And besides, Big Dick will get out and look for me again. Only this time, I'll have gotten him arrested as well.

No. I need to find a way to…

And then it hits me—TwatKnot. He'd put his number into my phone. He was a Black Hood, and the Black Hoods were famous for helping people, especially from terrifying psychopaths like Big Dick.

I hit another stop sign then, and the pedestrians crossing the street block my path. Big Dick pulls up behind me, a grin on his face as his front tire bumps my rear bumper hard enough to make the car jolt forward just a bit.

Pulling up my contacts, I find his name and make the call.

Chapter 13

TWATKNOT

THE CROWD GOES wild as three bikes come ripping down the track for the speed races. I peer up from V's bike in the pits as they roar by us. V goes stiff next to me. Fucker's scared, as he should be. Most of the guys on this track are seasoned riders. Some even ride professionally.

"You sure you want to go through with this?" Priest asks. "Not too late to back out."

V thaws just enough to shake his head. "What class was that again?"

"Amateur class." I almost laugh when V gulps hard. "That was just the first heat. There are three more before yours," I remind him.

Priest slaps him on the shoulder. "Dude, you got this."

V relaxes slightly, returning to his bike and the pre-rally tune-up. When V steps away, his back to us, Priest looks over at me and drags his thumb across his neck. It takes all I have to stifle a laugh, because Priest is right. V's in trouble, but I have to commend him for even trying. I sure as hell wouldn't have signed up for a rally race, and not in front of our entire club, who are either lining the stands or walking through the pits.

Helping V do a few final checks, I feel my phone vibrating in my pocket. Pulling it out, I frown at the local number, but I'm curious, so I answer.

"Hello?"

"TK?" I recognize Cora's voice instantly, even though it's shaky and rushed. "I'm in trouble. I need help."

I step away from the crew. "What's going on?"

"I–I," she stammers, her voice filled with panic. "I don't know how to explain it."

I motion to the others and head off toward the exit. "Where are you?"

"I'm in my car."

"That tells me what you're in, but not where, gorgeous."

"On Kincaid, just off the main street. I'm… not alone."

I stop dead in my tracks. V and Priest are right behind me, and they halt too as I say, "Cora, talk to me. Tell me what's going on."

"I don't know," she mutters. "I don't know." A soft

voice echoes in the background, but I can't make out the words. "I think he's following me."

"Who's following you?"

"A man…"

"Listen to me, sweetheart. Take a deep breath and tell me exactly where you are." She rattles something off, but between the roaring of the motorcycle race behind me, and the street noise on her end, I can't hear a damn thing. "I'm gonna need you to say that again."

"I'm close to the bar!" she yells. "My bar."

"Can you get inside and lock the doors?"

"No, I don't have the keys. I don't know what to do, TK. I can't go home, 'cause then he'll know where I live."

Shit. Shit. Shit. Think, asshole. My bike's at least a ten-minute walk away on the other side of the track, less if I run, but that few minutes isn't going to help either of us.

"I'm not far away, but it's going to take me too long to get to you. Do you know where Full Throttle's race track is?"

"Yes," she replies quickly.

"Good, sweetheart. I want you to get here as fast as you can. Speed if you have to, and I'll meet you in the parking lot."

Her voice sounds even shakier when she replies, "Okay."

"I'm not hanging up, Cora. I'll stay with you the entire way. Just keep talking and drive straight to me."

I mute the line.

"Get the guys," I order. "Now! Have them meet me at the entrance."

"On it." V grabs Priest and they take off running toward the track.

Making my way to the parking lot, I take my phone off mute and place it back to my ear. "Tell me where you're at now." She says a street name, and I pretend to know where it's at. I don't know Sturgis like she does, but if I tell her that, she'll only panic more. I have to keep her calm.

"Is he still behind you?"

"Yes."

I pick up the pace, skidding around the corner of a concession stand near the bleachers just inside the track, and the parking lot comes into view.

"Do you see the track entrance yet?"

"I think so… Yes! Yes, I see it."

"Come straight up to the ticket booth. Don't stop for anything until you see me. My club and I will be there waiting."

I reach the booth a minute later, the brothers already coming up behind me.

"What the fuck's goin' on?" Judge asks me.

"Cora. Someone's following her car. I told her to come here."

Judge's nostrils flare, and the guys go on alert. Stone-

Face cracks his knuckles, likely excited at the idea of crushing some heads.

"I just pulled into the parking lot," she informs me. I look toward the entrance as a cloud of dust from the dirt road plumes into the air. A small sedan is barreling toward us, with a motorcycle hot on its tail.

"I see you. Keep coming, you're almost here."

I wave my arms as she approaches, and her wild eyes lock onto mine as she brings her car to a skidding halt, just to the left of us. She isn't even fully stopped when I run to her driver's side door and yank it open. Her hands tremble as she attempts to unbuckle her seatbelt.

I reach in and release the latch. "You're safe, gorgeous. I've got you now." She doesn't look at me, but at the little dark-haired boy in the back seat. My eyes nearly bug out when I see him. He looks terrified.

"My son. Get my son," she whispers.

"I've got him." I shift away from the door. "Get her out," I order. StoneFace steps forward, switching spots with me while I move to the other side of the car. The little boy stares up at me, his eyes wide and his face pale as I reach inside.

"Hey, little man. I'm just gonna get you out of your seat, okay?"

I fumble with the buckle, and when it releases, I put my hands under his arms and scoop him up. His tiny arms wrap around my neck at the same time Cora gets out of her seat. She runs toward us and plucks him from my arms, hugging him close to her chest.

"You're okay, baby. You're okay." He snuggles against her chest, but doesn't say a word. I'm so focused on the two of them, I almost miss the roar of a Harley pulling up right next to us. Cora stiffens. "That's him," she whispers against her son's head.

"Stay here."

I glare at the middle-aged man staring at us all from his motorcycle. He eyes our crowd, and I zero in on his cut, committing what I can see of his patch to memory.

"Hey, asshole, you and I need to have a chat." I stalk toward him, but he twists the throttle and takes off before I reach him. The cloud of dust follows him through the line of cars and back toward the exit.

"Do we follow?" someone asks from behind me, but I know it's pointless. That fucker will be long gone before we can get to our bikes.

I turn back, going right to Cora and the little boy. "He's gone."

"Thank you." Our eyes lock, and what feels like a spark of electricity flows between us. We stay like that, staring at each other, until her son squirms in her arms and she takes a step back, clearing her throat. "I'm sorry to have bothered you. I tried to call my parents, but they didn't answer. The police would've taken forever to get there. I didn't know what to do or who else to call."

"I'm glad you called me, Cora." And I am. I can't imagine what that fucker had planned for her, but whatever it was, he'll have to go through me first.

"Who are you?" the little boy in her arm asks, his big brown eyes looking at me curiously.

I give him a smile. "My name is Jonas. I'm a friend of your mom's." She blinks hard. Whether that reaction is to me giving him my real name or us being friends, I don't know. When the boy doesn't say any more, I return my attention to his mother. "Tell me what happened."

"That bad man tried to talk to my momma," her son informs me. "He scared her."

I frown. "Do you know this guy, Cora?"

"I—" A phone rings inside of her car, stopping her from finishing. "Shit, that's probably my parents." She shifts her son and goes to grab it.

Setting him down, she opens the passenger side door to retrieve her phone. Holding it to her ear, she coos, "Hi, Dad... No... No... No, I'm okay," she says. She holds up a finger, asking for a second.

Karma approaches me while she's distracted. "Did you know she had a kid?"

"No fucking clue, man."

"Does that change things?"

I frown. "There'd have to be something there to change. The last time I saw her, she was leaving the bar and didn't look back."

He claps a hand to my shoulder. "She called *you*, man," he points out. "There's something fucking there."

I shake my head, curious at the excitement that idea brings to me. "I was just the last choice she had. She didn't know who else to call."

Karma smirks. "Lindsey wasn't kidding. You really don't know a damn thing about women, do you?"

"Your girl has a big mouth," I mutter. Client confidentiality, my ass. Though I'm not technically a client, per se. "Did she just tell you, or does the entire club know?"

"Oh, we all know, but it wasn't Lindsey who told us —it was you. I may have been drunk as a fucking skunk at that concert, but I heard everything you said, and saw her reaction too," he admits. "I'm surprised she hasn't cut your balls off yet, to be honest."

"Fuck you," I retort, but there's no fire behind it, because he's right. I deserve to have my balls cut off for the way I had made her look at me that night. I'd fucking crushed her.

"Admit it," he chuckles. "That woman's gotten underneath your skin."

While she finishes up her call, I think about his words.

One minute, I'm making friends with the cute little badass bartender on our first night here, only to insult her and then beg for forgiveness. Now I'm her savior. It's enough to give me fucking whiplash. And then I realize it—Karma is right.

Cora has gotten underneath my skin. Admitting that to myself is hard enough, but admitting it to Karma was not fucking happening today.

Chapter 14

CORA

"IT'S OKAY, HONESTLY," I say, pulling Harrison from his seat and placing him on the sidewalk. "My mom and dad will be home soon. Besides, Big Dick doesn't know where I live, and there's no way he followed me here with my leather entourage."

TK shakes his head. "I don't feel comfortable just leaving you. We're gonna stick around, at least until your parents get home."

I look past him to the others, but they've already parked their motorcycles and are walking toward us. My cheeks burn as I meet his eyes once again. "TK, for real. You guys don't have to stay."

He shifts his attention to Harrison. "Your mom's very stubborn."

Giggling, Harrison nods his head in agreement and

grabs TK's hand, dragging him up to the house. "Wanna see my race cars?"

TK looks back at me and answers, "Absolutely."

Emotions war inside my mind, freezing me in place. Why is he doing this? Him and the Black Hoods scared Big Dick off, for now, so why is he still here helping the fat, mouthy bartender?

"Momma, unlock the door," Harrison demands from the front step.

"Yeah, Momma," the one named V drawls, "Let us in."

The group of enormous men and their women standing in front of my house has me grinning at how ridiculous they all look. Stalking toward the door, Harrison shoves past me as soon as it's unlocked, pulling TK with him.

"Come to my room! I'll show you."

"Got any beer?" V asks, stepping through the door.

"Kitchen fridge." My eyes widen as the group piles inside, leaving me alone on my own front step. *What the fuck is happening?*

A beautiful brunette smiles at me from the foyer and motions for me to come in. "Welcome to the insanity," she says with a laugh. "Once one of the boys takes a liking to you, you're forever tethered to the rest of us."

"Oh, it's not like that," I assure her, closing the door behind me. "I just didn't know who else to call."

The woman assesses me. "How'd you get his number?"

"He put it in my phone."

She nods knowingly. "Oh, honey, it's definitely like that. My name is Lindsey, by the way. The big one with the name Karma on his patch is mine."

I'm at a loss for words, so all I say is, "Cora. Nice to meet you."

I make my way into the kitchen and am surprised to find the ladies already in there. I can see the men out on the back deck through the patio doors. What the hell?

"Momma," Harrison squeals, entering the kitchen with TK's hand still in his. "We're going out back. Jonas is gonna check out my treehouse."

I look at TK. "You're going into a treehouse?"

He nods, but says nothing. Harrison leads the way outside, with TK hot on his heels. As soon as the door closes behind them, all of us burst out laughing.

"Oh, I gotta get this on video," Lindsey says, moving toward the door. "A six foot six man climbing up a ladder into some little treehouse? It'll go viral in a heartbeat."

The rest of us head outside and watch as first Harrison, then TK, then V, Priest, and even Karma climb the wooden ladder into Harrison's treehouse.

"It's like a clown car," Lindsey howls, her camera recording every hilarious second.

"Cora?" I turn to find Judge, the MC president, standing just behind me. "Wonder if I can have a word?"

Suddenly nervous, I follow Judge through the patio doors and back into my kitchen.

Once we're alone, he leans against the counter and folds his arms over his chest. "I couldn't help but notice the president patch on that man's cut. What would the president of an MC want with you?"

Sighing, I take a seat in the closest chair. I don't want to lie to the president of the Black Hoods MC, but I also don't want to tell him the real reason Big Dick was trying to corner me. "I haven't seen him for years," I admit. "But he may have heard some things that made him want to talk to me, but I don't want to talk to him, ever."

Judge's jaw hardens as he stares at me. I expect him to ask more questions, but he doesn't. Instead, he nods. "Beef with another club is a big deal, young lady. TK's putting his neck and ours on the line for you, so that tells me you mean something to him. Make sure you remember that."

I gape at him, shocked. I'd never thought about that. Big Dick is the president of a very dangerous MC. What will that mean for the Black Hoods now that they've stood up for me?

"Cora?" my mother's voice calls out from the front hall. "Why on earth are there so many bikers in my—" She enters the kitchen at that moment and spots Judge.

"Oh, hello." Her eyes dart to mine. "Is everything okay here, Cora?"

Bless her. My momma is a wildcat. If I told her that no, things weren't okay, she'd throw Judge out herself, right on his ass. But thankfully, she doesn't have to. "Yes, Momma, it's good. This is…" I pause, unsure of how to introduce him.

Stepping forward, Judge offers my mother his hand. "Name's Judge," he says. Momma accepts his hand and gives it a tentative shake. I can tell she's dazzled by him. Hell, I'm twenty years younger, and Judge dazzles me.

"Nice to meet you, Judge," she breathes.

Laughter erupts on the back deck, and we all turn to see my father, standing in the center of them all, telling one of his stories, complete with wild hand gestures. At some point during our conversation, TK and the others had climbed back down and were now being held captive by my father.

I watch as he holds up a finger, and then opens the sliding glass door. "Lynne, get the burgers and hot dogs out of the freezer. We have guests for dinner."

I look past him and my eyes meet TK's. Butterflies flip and twirl inside my belly at just that simple look.

And then he winks.

God help me.

Chapter 15

TWATKNOT

IF YOU HAD TOLD me this morning that me and the club would be having an impromptu cookout with Cora's family, I'd have said you were crazy. Yet, here we stand in the back yard of her parents' house with the grill fired up and music playing.

"You want a hot dog or a hamburger?" Cora's dad asks with his oven mitt covered hand, waving around a spatula.

"Burger," I say, then lean in and speak a little more quietly. "I apologize for invading your space here. We just didn't want to leave Cora and the kid alone until you were here."

"Pay it no mind. You boys helped my family today. It's the least we can do to thank you."

"It was nothing, sir," I offer politely.

"Sir?" he chuckles. "Call me Jim."

He takes a swig of his beer and returns to his work on the grill. Cora's mom comes out of the house with two large bowls, balancing a plate on top of them. Lindsey spies her balancing act and sprints over to help by grabbing the plate and walking with her to the patio table.

Cora stands nearby, watching Harrison toss a ball back and forth with Grace and Delilah.

Taking in the scene, I can't hold back my wistful sigh. I miss this, having a family that loves you.

My childhood had been pretty normal. Well, as normal as it could be, seeing as I was the misfit son of the local pastor. My parents had loved me as fiercely as Cora seems to love her son and parents.

When I joined the MC, they just didn't understand, and I hadn't tried to make them. Though we didn't talk much more than a few times a year around the holidays, part of me still knows they ignore this part of my life completely, wishing it out of existence as their way to ignore my life choices.

"Between you and me," her father says, pulling me from my thoughts, "arriving home and seeing all these bikers at my house freaked me the hell out."

I can't help but laugh. "I can certainly understand why it would. When I asked a couple of the guys to help me escort her home, I didn't expect them all to come."

"My wife and I appreciate what you did for Cora, but I have to know, who are you to my daughter?"

I pause, considering it. "To be honest, Jim, I don't really know how to answer that. I'd like to call Cora a friend, but I don't even think she likes me much."

Jim throws his head back and laughs. "You wouldn't be the first man to wonder about that, I'm afraid. It does make me curious, though, why you came out in full force to help her if you don't even know if she's your friend?"

I have to give him credit. The man is not afraid of confrontation.

"When she called me, scared out of her fucking mind, what she is to me didn't matter. She needed help." The way her voice had lost all sense of her confidence will haunt me the rest of my life. "Seeing her that scared, scared me. I didn't think she was afraid of anything."

Jim nods knowingly. "Cora's a special kind of woman."

I nod in agreement. "I watched her manhandle a grown ass man out of her bar, as if he were no bigger than a toddler. Just carried on her conversation as she tossed his ass out the door."

Jim peers over at his daughter. "She gets it from her mother," he smirks. "Lynne was just like her in high school. Half the football team steered clear of her after she kicked the ass of one of them who had spread a rumor about her. He lives a few blocks down the road, and I swear he still gives her a wide berth all these years later."

I raise my brow. "That five foot nothing woman did that?"

He smiles wide. "And then some."

How had this man survived in a household with two badass women under the same roof all these years? My respect for him grows by the second.

Suddenly, the air changes around us, a heaviness encompassing us both.

Jim leans in, his voice almost a whisper when he says, "Cora's got a history. It's not my story to tell, and I don't even know you, but I will say this—she's strong. An immovable force once she sets her mind to something, but she's far from invincible."

Fuck. She told him about what I said at the concert. No wonder if I'm getting a new boyfriend once-over from her dad? "Jim, I don't know what she told you—" I start to say before Judge joins us.

"You don't have to worry about that, Jim. From what I've seen of your daughter over the last few days, we should be warning her not to hurt him. She could wipe the floor with this guy." He jerks his head toward me and grins. "In fact, I'd pay good money to see that."

Jim chuckles. "Me too."

"It's too bad we're pulling out tomorrow," Judge

continues. "I enjoy seeing this asshole get his balls handed to him day in and day out."

Raising his brow, Jim looks at me with something close to disapproval. "Heading out, you say?"

"Wait, what?" Cora walks over to the three of us, her face unreadable, but I could've sworn I'd just seen a flash of sadness before she reached us. "You're leaving? All of you?"

Judge nods. "The rally has a few more days left, but our kids are back in Texas. It's been a nice trip, but it's time we head back home."

"Texas? That's a bit of a ways from here," Jim notes, his gaze focused on his daughter.

"Tell me about it. Nineteen hours on a Harley at my age?" Judge guffaws, rubbing the back of his neck. "I feel it the next day, and the day after that."

"I feel it every morning when I get out of bed," Jim counters.

Judge and Jim fall deeper into conversation about whatever it is old men talk about, excluding Cora and I. I peer over at her and tip my head to the side, inviting her to talk somewhere else. Smiling, she leads me to a bench at the far side of the yard, giving us some privacy.

Settling in next to each other, she tilts her head toward me and asks, "Why didn't you tell me you were leaving tomorrow?"

"*They're* leaving."

That has her perking up. "You're not going with them?"

"Not sure yet." Rubbing my hands together, I inquire, "We're all going to grab breakfast in the morning before they leave. Would you like to come?"

Her smile grows wide. "It's a date."

Chapter 16

CORA

STEPPING into Greta's Breakfast Bar and Mexican Cantina, I scan over the tables, looking for the group. I haven't been here in years, but I'm not surprised to see that nothing has changed.

"Well, well, well," Greta Titsworth crows in her thick, Wisconsin accent. "Haven't seen that pretty face around here in a long time."

I take in the tall brunette owner of the restaurant and smile. I'd always liked Greta, even though her eyes always seemed to linger just a little too long on my chest. "Hey, girl. How have you been?"

"I've lost thirty pounds. My girls still sit where they should—" she puffs out her chest, "—and I almost have the sleeve completed on my arm."

I take in the colorful tattoos adorning nearly every inch of her porcelain skin. "Wow. Those are incredible."

"I know. If you're ever looking to get one, I can get you in with my guy on a friends and family discount. You just let me know." She winks. "Now, you here alone or meetin' somebody?"

Over her shoulder, I see TK approaching. "Meeting somebody."

Turning, she takes in TK and all his gorgeous physique. "Holy shit, girl. You ridin' that baloney pony?"

"Well?" he teases, stopping next to her. "Answer her."

Greta looks at me and arches her brow, knowing she's got me.

"No, I'm not riding that baloney pony," I grouse, rolling my eyes.

TK bursts into laughter, and Greta's shoulders shake with mirth, always happy to make someone squirm. I try to squeeze past her, but she grabs my arm and tells me, "You make him work for it, baby girl." With that, she releases me and scurries off to mortify another paying customer.

"She's quite the character," TK notes, leading me to the back of the restaurant where the group has pulled a number of tables together to fit them all.

"She's crazy," I tell him.

As we approach, TK rushes around me and pulls out

an empty chair for me to sit in. *Who knew bikers were chivalrous?*

"Hey, Cora," Lindsey coos, followed by greetings from the rest of them.

"Hi, everyone." Taking my seat, I gape up at TK when he pushes it in for me, then drops into the chair next to mine.

Picking up the menu, I browse through the options as the boys talk about the long trip home, and about someone named GP whose ass Judge wants to kick. But even as I try to take in what they're saying, my head swims with TK's proximity.

His bicep brushes against mine every time he moves, and his scent of deodorant, soap, and a mild, musky cologne is intoxicating.

Fat, mouthy bartender.

He's just being nice, Cora. Don't get attached.

Just then, TK looks over at me and smiles. "You look great today."

Fat, mouthy bartender.

I smile at his unnecessary politeness and look away, joining the conversation the girls are having about dreading their asses falling asleep on the motorcycles.

TK's hand comes down to rest on my knee, causing heat to pool between my legs. When his thumb swipes back and forth on my bare skin, my heart takes off at a gallop.

He leans forward, his lips in my hair, and whispers, "You look better than great. You look fucking gorgeous."

My breath hitches in my throat. Turning toward him, his eyes stare into mine with far more intensity than I was expecting at a breakfast table full of hungry bikers. "Thank you."

His eyes drop to my lips and we stay that way, frozen, our noses barely an inch apart.

"Jesus," Karma mutters from the other end of the table. "Get a room."

Lindsey swats his arm, but the mood is already broken. Well, kind of.

The waitress comes and takes our orders, and for the next forty-five minutes, I forget that I just met these people. For the first time in a long time, I feel like I have actual friends. Hell, for the first time in forever, I feel like I have *actual* friends.

But even though I'm eating delicious food with great people, I can't help but tremble every time TK's arm brushes against mine.

Judge looks from TK to Priest. "So, you boys are both staying back?"

TK nods, and Priest sighs loudly. "Can't leave a brother behind."

"Ah, come on, man," TK teases, leaning over to look at Priest on the other side of me. "It'll be fun. A bros weekend."

Priest sneers and says to Judge, "Please tell me there's more than one room booked?"

Chuckling, Judge throws Priest a keycard. "You can have mine and Grace's room, but I'll warn ya, TK's staying in the room right next to yours, where Lindsey and Karma were staying, and you can hear *everything*."

"Right on!" Hashtag whoops. "Bet ya liked that, hey, Prez?"

Karma glares at him, and Judge curls his lip in disgust.

"You guys have a room now?" I ask, my brows raised in surprise. "What happened to roughing it?"

Priest snorts, and TK flips him the bird. "Just thought if we're gonna stay, we may as well do it in style."

I don't know if I would call the Sturgis Motel style, but it beats a tent in a crowded campground, I suppose.

Before I know it, the check arrives, and Judge pays for everyone's meal. And then, as one very large, very loud group, we head outside. I toss Greta a wave as I pass, and she winks and gives me a wicked grin while motioning to TK.

"See you boys in a few days," Judge says once everyone has said their goodbyes. "You take care of these boys for me, Cora. Lord knows, they'll get into trouble on their own."

I step up to the fatherly biker and pull him in for a

hug. "I'll do my best," I promise, and take a step back. "Drive safe."

In a roar of exhaust and thrilling throttle twists, the group disappears down the road, leaving Priest, TK and me on the sidewalk.

Suddenly, my nerves take hold, and I know I need to get out of here. Just yesterday, I had been plotting TK's death for the words he'd said about me, and today, I'm hanging out with him like it never happened.

"Well, I have to go get Harrison off to summer camp. Thanks for breakfast, gentleman."

Before TK can stop me, I give them a quick wave and rush to my car. My mother had taken Harrison to camp over an hour ago, but after that breakfast, I need space. Space from TK and his intoxicating smell. Space from thinking about how much I want to climb him like a tree. And most of all, space from having to decide if I can forget what he sees and thinks of me.

Chapter 17

TWATKNOT

HOT WATER from the shower head beats down on my back like molten lava. After nearly a week in a tent, this shower, and that king-size bed teasing me from the other room, are a welcome bonus of opting to stay put for a few more days. Taking a deep breath, I lean my head against the wall, letting my thoughts drift.

Cora's face flashes through my mind. Her smiling as she laughed at one of V's lame ass jokes. The flush of her cheeks when I'd ran my thumb over the smooth skin of her knee.

Seeing her with my club, in my world, had stirred something in me. Something new. Unexpected. And her ass in the fucking shorts she'd worn this morning? *Jesus.*

My cock stirs at the thought. Wrapping my hand around my hardening length, I squeeze, pumping once.

The sensation nearly lifts me up on my toes, forcing a

hiss from between my teeth. I shouldn't be thinking about her like this, but she's all I can think about, so I pump again, losing myself in the motion.

Suddenly, a sharp knock echoes through my motel room.

At first, I ignore it, touching myself again, but the knock comes a second time, only louder.

"Ah, for fuck's sake." Slipping from the shower, I turn it off. "I'll be back," I mutter to both myself and to it. Only pausing to grab a towel from the rack and wrapping it around my hips, I trudge toward the incessant noise that won't stop.

"Someone better be fucking dead, Priest," I yell, yanking open the door. "I was fucking busy—"

But it's not Priest—it's Cora.

"Uh, hi." Her wide eyes trail along my naked torso, pausing when they reach the towel haphazardly wrapped around my waist.

"You're not Priest," I purr.

Cora doesn't respond. She seems frozen in place, and I follow her gaze, realizing just what she's staring at. "Fuck, hang on." Slightly closing the door, I go in search of my jeans, finding them thrown over the bed. It takes me a minute to tug them over my wet legs, but I get it done.

Once the bottom half of me is covered, I return to the door, where Cora seems cemented on the other side.

"Come in, please," I say, moving aside for her to enter.

Cora's teeth sink into her lower lip. I'm sure she's about to bolt, but finally, she snaps out of it and steps inside, closing the door behind her. I consider asking her to sit down, but the only option would be the bed. She already looks ready to run out of the room as it is, and the offer would likely have her running for the hills.

Though the raging arousal that's been building up inside of me would very much like it if she sat there and let me make her mine.

"I was just in the shower," I inform her, as if she couldn't tell.

"I, uh… I noticed." Her face is a delicious pink that makes her look even more beautiful. How did I not see how gorgeous she is? "I should've texted or called first, not shown up unannounced."

"It's fine, Cora." Her usual unwavering confidence and sharp tongue are nowhere to be seen, but her eyes are still fixed on my bare torso. "Did you want something, or did you just come for the view?"

"I—" Her mouth hangs open in surprise as she tries to collect her thoughts enough to say something witty like she usually does. "I wasn't even looking," she lies, snapping her hand over her mouth.

Caught red-handed, darlin'.

"So you have a habit of showing up unannounced to

a man's motel room?" Grinning, I fold my arms over my chest. "You continue to surprise me, Cora."

"No... I mean... Goddammit! Why is it so hard to talk to you?" She wrings her hands, and I find myself enjoying her obvious discomfort. "I came here because I want to apologize to you."

I blink at her, confused. "Apologize? For what, exactly?"

She looks down at the floor now, her tone serious. "For the way I've treated you the last few days."

Reaching out, I tuck a tendril of her long, dark hair behind her ear. "You don't owe me anything, sweetheart. After what I said about you..." I shake my head, thoroughly ashamed. "I deserved every fucking second of your anger, and then some."

She steps forward, close enough that I can smell her floral perfume. The scent is intoxicating, and I forget all about the arguments we've had and the nasty words we've exchanged. All I can think about is her hair loose around her shoulders like it is, and she's still wearing those fucking shorts.

Get it together, asshole.

Her magnetic brown eyes look intensely into mine, scattering my thoughts. All I can think about is this woman.

Before I have a chance to even think about what I'm doing, my hand shoots out and grips the back of her neck, pulling her toward me. My lips come down and claim hers, sending me soaring.

I don't often kiss the women I have sex with. Kissing has never been high on my list of things that rev my engine. But in this moment, that all changes, because Cora's lips, and the softness of her body pressed against mine, consume me.

I want more. I need more. I want to get closer. I don't even know if I can get close enough.

And then her fingers come up and twirl through my hair, gripping it tightly at the nape of my neck, and I know there's no turning back.

CORA

MY HEART SPUTTERS in my chest. Squeezing my eyes closed, I press my body closer to his. His chest is bare, still covered in droplets of water from his shower. My fingertips rest on his shoulder, and then move lower, over his chest and down along his washboard stomach.

His body is pure perfection. Equal parts hard, and as soft as the most expensive silk.

"God, Cora," he mutters. Tearing his lips from mine, he trails searing hot kisses along the side of my neck. "You smell so fucking good."

My head spins and I gasp, sucking in air. *How did we get to this?*

My train of thought disappears in an instant when his hands grip the hem of my T-shirt and whisk it up over my head.

My lightheaded swooning screeches to a halt.

Suddenly, I feel exposed. Uncertain. I'd already heard his thoughts on my body, and here I am, standing in front of him in nothing but a purple lace bra and a pair of jean shorts.

I pause, pulling away. I can't do this.

"Cora," he whispers, his eyes trailing along my half-naked frame. "Fuck, you're gorgeous."

He reaches for me again, this time with his large hand cupping my ass and pulling me into his rock-hard arousal. He gives me a quick kiss, and he's gone.

I watch in awe as he drops to his knees, his eyes on my lace-covered chest, hungry with need. He leans forward and kisses the top of one breast, and then the other. Snaking his hand around my back, he undoes my bra, leaving it to hang loosely at my shoulders.

I don't dare move as he glides it down my arms and tosses it to the floor behind him. He looks up and any insecurities I'd felt about being naked in front of this man melt away.

His eyes are dark and hooded, filled with so much desire. "Cora," he groans. He doesn't say the words, but I know he's asking my permission. He's telling me that if I give it, nothing between us will ever be the same.

My chest rises and falls as I take in his beautiful face, until finally, I fist the back of his hair and pull him to my breast while arching my back.

He moans against my skin, his tongue swirling

around one nipple, and then the other.

God, he feels so good.

Closing my eyes, I drop my head back, reveling in the feel of his mouth on me.

Grazing his teeth over my left nipple, I gasp. "Eyes on me," he instructs. "Always."

I stare down at him, dragging air into my lungs, my face twisted in sweet agony as he ravishes them, leaving no part of them untouched with his lips and tongue.

"These fucking shorts... You have no idea what they did to me at breakfast." He pops the button and slowly drags them down my shaking legs. "Fucking beautiful," he breathes, pressing his lips to my mound.

Once my shorts are on the floor, he places a hand on my ankle and raises it until my foot is resting on his knee. I shudder as he presses a kiss to the inside of my thigh, only to repeat the process with the other.

My body trembles beneath his touch. I don't even know what I need from him at this point, but goddammit, I need it right fucking now.

Skimming his nose along my inner thigh, he makes his way to my center. "Smells so fucking good," I hear him say.

Releasing my legs, he comes up and kisses me while fumbling with his zipper.

Nipping my lip, he rids himself of his jeans, giving me my first look at his impressive cock.

"I want you so fucking bad, Cora. Just say the word, and I'll stop right now."

Am I ready for this? Do I *want* this?

Fuck yes, I want this.

Instead of saying the words, I roll my bottom lip between my teeth while running a single finger along his length from base to tip.

"Jesus."

Wrapping his hands around my waist, he turns me toward the bed and pushes my chest into the mattress, leaving me with my ass in the air. I can feel him behind me, hear the crinkling of a condom wrapper, and then his cock poking at my entrance. In one swift thrust, he buries himself as far as he can go, and I can't help the cry of pleasure that escapes past my lips.

"Fuck," he grinds out through clenched teeth, pulling out slowly and gliding back in.

Moaning, I push back, wanting more of him. All of him. Every fucking delicious inch of him.

"I'm sorry, baby, but this is gonna be quick," he warns. "You're fucking killing me."

"Fuck me," I tell him, pressing my ass against him and rolling my hips. I can already feel my release building, and I need it so bad.

Digging his fingertips into my hip, he uses his other hand to wrap around my throat, pulling me up until my back meets his chest. His lips press against my ear, and I can hear his heavy breathing as he moves faster, his hips finding a rhythm, his skin slapping against mine.

"You feel so fucking good, Cora." His hand tightens around my throat, just a little. "Show me how you touch yourself, baby."

I wrap a hand around his wrist at my throat, surprised at how wanted the act makes me feel, and allow the other to trail down along my belly and to my center. I can feel his massive length plunging in and out as I collect the wetness we're making together on the tip of my finger.

"I'm gonna come," I tell him.

"Touch your pussy, Cora. Show me how you make yourself feel good."

My fingertip glides over my already swollen nub, and TK hisses, his hips moving faster, his body bending us both forward.

"Touch it."

I roll my finger around in circles, my fingertip building me up to an almost unbearable level, and I can feel my pussy tightening around him.

Releasing my hip, he slaps my ass, just hard enough to sting, and I fall.

My release hits me like a tidal wave, washing over me with pleasure so intense, I forget where I am. I cry out and moan, my coherent mind washing away with the rest of me. His grip tightening on my throat, I hear him roar as he attempts to hold my hips still, but I can't stop myself from rolling them, trying to ride my orgasm for as long as I can.

Moments later, our bodies go still while we gasp for air. TK slowly pulls out of me and steps away.

Oh, fuck. What have I done?

He chuckles softly at something unsaid before disappearing into the bathroom.

As soon as I hear the water running, I grab my panties and shorts and scramble into them. My bra is on the other side of the bed. As soon as I get it clasped, I'm pulling down my T-shirt just as TK comes out of the bathroom, a wet face cloth in his hand and a smile on his face.

That smile fades instantly when he sees that I'm dressed.

"What are you d—"

"I gotta go," I say, my hand reaching for the doorknob. "I have to—"

I have to do nothing, but since I can't think of anything else to say, I shake my head, whip open the door, and rush outside.

I leave TK naked, standing in the doorway to the bathroom, an expression full of confusion.

What the fuck was I thinking?

Letting TK pity fuck me might've felt good in the moment, but I have never felt more ashamed.

Chapter 19

TWATKNOT

I STARE at the closed door in disbelief. She's gone. She'd just fucking left, like what we had just done didn't mean shit.

Fuck.

This is what I've been doing. This is karma coming to kick my stupid ass for every transgression I've ever made in my life. My pastor father would be happy to know that my choices are finally catching up to me now that I've found Cora. He'd be reveling in my misery right now.

I've been plowing my way through the female population like they're nothing, breaking hearts and spirits. I certainly never treated any of them as human beings with feelings or desires of their own. Is this how I'd made them feel? Did I leave them with this hollow ache in the pit of their stomachs when they woke up in the morning and I was gone, no number left on the night-stand or plans to see them again?

I'd fucked them and chucked them without a second thought, then returned to the clubhouse and told the tales of my exploits to the guys like proud war stories.

I'm a fucking monster.

Dread, rage, and disappointment fight for dominance inside of me.

Was this how she felt too? Or was this about what I'd said at that concert, making her doubt whether or not my feelings were genuine?

I'd done this to myself. Until Cora, I'd been drifting in the wind, more than happy to do this to any woman with an interest in me.

Cora walked out, though, and that changes every-thing. Maybe this is the wake-up call I didn't even know I needed.

Cora's face passes through my mind like a movie. The beautiful smile when I made her laugh. Her capti-vating blush when I pissed her off. The way her lips had parted when I'd plunged inside of her sweet heat.

I've had some amazing sexual partners, but they've all amounted to nothing when compared to her. There's only one Cora, the beautiful, mouthy bartender, who made me *feel* something after all these years. The woman I'd just let walk out of this room without a word.

Go after her, fucker.

Maybe it would be better to just pack up my shit and hit the road, but the thought of it makes me sick to my stomach. It would be no better than what I've done so many other times before.

Fuck that. I'm not doing that to Cora.

I want to know why she came to my motel room and let me touch her sweet body? And then I want to know why she left? I guess the only way I'm going to get any answers is to go after her.

My confidence is shaken for the first time in my life. I've never second-guessed any of my decisions about women until now—until Cora.

I consider it all. Could I live with not trying?

I felt something, and she felt it too—I know she did.

The feeling as she came around my cock felt like home. I want that and so much more.

I'm only a few steps away from the door when there's a knock, and relief washes over me.

Cora's back.

I throw open the door, only to hear the housekeeper scream, her eyes bugging out of her head. Even the old lady from across the hall is as shocked as the housekeeper to see my naked ass panting in the doorway. I peer left and right down the hall, but there's no Cora in sight.

"Did you see a woman leave here?"

"No!" the housekeeper squeaks. "Sir, your clothes!"

She averts her eyes before making a mad dash down the hall. The older lady clutches the pearls around her neck, but hasn't once looked away.

I nod to her before closing the door. "Ma'am." As the lock clicks into place, I rest my head against the cool wood before slamming my fists into it. The pain radiates through my wrists, all the way up my arms. I'm pretty sure I might've cracked a knuckle or two, but it's nothing compared to what's raging inside of me.

If it's a chase she wants, I'll fucking give it to her.

First step? Show her what she's missing out on if she walks away from temptation at its finest, and a misguided use of my religious upbringing to use to my advantage. My dad would be *so* proud of me.

Spinning on my heel, I go straight to my bag. Not having access to a washing machine while camping bites me in the ass when I dig through the mostly wrinkled clothes. T-shirts, all black. *Fuck.* I need something better, but finding something that isn't black, leather, or bike related in Sturgis will be difficult. I'd seen that for myself when Judge had me out shopping with the ladies.

Think, dumbass. Think!

A grin spreads across my lips when I realize my salvation might just be next door. We're about the same size, or close enough to it.

Shoving myself into a clean pair of jeans and donning my black riding boots, I grab my wallet, keys, and phone, and stuff them into my pockets. Lastly, I grab my cut and storm out of the room. I have to knock a few times before Priest finally answers, eyeing me up and down.

"If you're looking for more of a good time, I think you've got the wrong room. The old lady is back that way."

"Heard that, huh?"

"I heard a lot of shit." No doubt he did. The walls were made thin in these older motels. I should apologize, but nah, I won't.

I push through the door and past him. "I need a shirt, one of those nice ones you have."

His brows raise in confusion. "Why?"

"Because I fucking asked for one."

Rolling his eyes, he heads to a duffle bag set out on the desk. Pulling out a few T-shirts, he tosses me a royal blue button-up shirt. "I'd like that back in one piece."

I pull it over my broad shoulders and button it up. Priest is a monster so the shirt hangs loose, but I button it up anyway. It'll have to do.

Throwing on my cut, I head over to the mirror on the wall and use my fingers to straighten up my hair. Satisfied with what I can do without hair gel, I stretch out my arms like a debutante doing her ballroom spin.

"How do I look?"

"Like you're wearing your daddy's fucking clothes."

"Fuck you."

"Please tell me you're not going to go propose to that girl just because you fucked her? I don't have the license to do that shit anymore. You know that, right?"

"Fuck off." But part of me kind of likes his little joke. Before, my insides would've shriveled right up at the mere mention of marriage. Now, with Cora, it's just intriguing.

"Care to enlighten me on what's going on, then? Because I have no fucking clue."

"I'm going after her."

He doesn't even flinch. Fucker knows she left. He probably heard her run out of my room. "And that requires one of my nicest shirts?"

"Yes!" I whine. What's so hard to understand?

Cora's seen the biker side of me, but I want her to see me like this. She has to know I'm more than just a biker —I'm a man. A man who can't seem to get enough of her.

Priest tips his head back and laughs. He laughs so hard he clutches his stomach, like I'd just said the funniest thing he's ever heard.

"The fuck you laughing for?"

"You're chasing after a woman!" he gasps between laughs. "Judge owes me a hundred when we get back. I knew it wouldn't take you more than a day."

I blink, sure I didn't hear that right. "You fuckers bet on us?"

"Hell yeah we did."

Of course they did. I should've known something was up when I spotted the group of them huddled around the bikes after breakfast like a bunch of school girls. Assholes, the whole lot of them.

"I hate all of you so much."

"Me and my hundred bucks are loving your ass right now." His eyes shine with excitement. "Oh, and the best part is, if she dumps your ass, I double my money."

I stalk past him, flipping him the bird on my way.

Gathering his phone and keys, Priest goes to follow me out.

"Where the fuck you think you're going?" I snarl.

"With you." His lips split into a wide grin as he passes me and opens the door. "Ain't no fucking way I'm missing this show."

CORA

"WHERE'S STELLA?" a man asks. I recognize him instantly as the dude that had been banging her in the boss's office a few days ago.

"She didn't show up today," I inform him, popping the caps off of three beer bottles and placing them on the waitress's tray. "Again."

The man frowns. "I was with her last night."

"Don't know what to tell ya. Stella hasn't been here for two weeks, and she's already missed three shifts. She's not exactly reliable, if ya know what I mean."

The biker ponders that a moment, his brow still creased, but I don't have time to sit around and discuss the many reasons he should steer clear of Stella. Because she didn't show up, I haven't had a moment to breathe all night.

Looking at the clock, I sigh. It's barely eleven, which

means the bar is open for another three hours, and I still have to clean up after that. I just want to go home, crawl into bed, and forget today even happened.

But I'll never forget today.

The memory of TK on his knees before me, his eyes on mine as he drew my nipple into his mouth, flashes through my mind. The way his hand had wrapped around my throat, both gentle and firm, claiming me in a way that no man has ever done, nor likely ever will again.

"Miss!"

I shake my head and focus, surprised I hadn't seen the middle-aged man standing right in front of me, clearly waiting for an answer to a question I hadn't heard him ask.

"I'm sorry. What was that?"

Holding up two fingers, he says, "Two Buds," and then returns to the conversation he'd been having with a tattooed woman with impressively high hair.

I grab the beers, pop the caps, and place them in front of him. Setting down a twenty-dollar bill, he saunters off.

Placing the money in the cash register, I make the change and drop that into my tip jar.

"Cora."

I turn at the sound of my name, half hoping to find TK, but instead it's Big Dick standing there. I swear, I've never been more thankful for the chest-high bar.

"I have nothing to say to you." I move to serve the next customer.

Moving down to serve the next customer, he opens his mouth to order, but Big Dick steps in and grabs him by the collar, pulling him close. I can't hear what he says, but I watch the man's face visibly pale as he bobs his head, agreeing with whatever he's being told.

As soon as Big Dick releases him, the man quickly disappears into the crowd.

"We need to talk," he says, placing both hands on the bar.

"I'm working."

"After work then," he insists.

"I can't."

Big Dicks chuffs out a humorless laugh and glares at another patron that attempts to approach. The man slinks away, apparently deciding he's not so thirsty after all.

"You owe me, Cora."

That does it for me. At that moment, I know exactly what people mean when they say they see red. How dare this motherfucker come into *my* town and *my* bar and tell *me* that I owe him a damn thing, especially after what *he* did to *me*.

I lean in close so I don't have to yell to be heard. "I don't owe you shit."

Nostrils flaring, his eyes flash with rage.

Just then, TK and Priest take up positions on either side, clamping their hands down on his shoulders and boxing him in against the bar top. I nearly sigh loudly in relief.

"Hey, fuckface," TK says in a cheerful tone. "I tried to talk to you yesterday, but you took off."

Big Dick jerks forward, his arms coming up as he tries to shake them off, but neither TK nor Priest release him.

"You were following Cora," Priest reminds him, "and now you're bugging her at work. We don't like that."

Big Dick turns and glares at Priest. "I don't care what you like. Now get your fucking hands off of me, or I'll have you dead before the sun comes up."

TK looks over at me and grins. "Oh, he's feisty. We like feisty."

"You boys have no idea who you're messing with."

"Sure we do. Your name's right there." TK pokes a finger into the patch on his cut. "Big Dick. So do they call you that because you *have* a big dick, or because you *are* a big dick?"

A vein throbs in Big Dick's temple, but both men are holding his arms down at his sides. He's not moving.

"I'm the fucking president of the Screwballs MC, assholes," he growls.

Looking over at Priest, TK's brows shoot up in mock surprise. "Oh, a president. Did you know this guy was a president?"

Priest's face stays stoic. "I did not."

TK yanks Big Dick toward him, placing his mouth near his ear, but I can still hear him when he says, "Well, Mr. President, since you're so important, we'll escort you outside instead of tossing you out on your ass."

It takes the two of them to pull Big Dick away from the bar, because he doesn't go quietly. The guys don't seem to be breaking a sweat, though. TK and Priest never waver, though. I can't tell you how much amusement I'm getting as they escort him out.

For just a second, I wonder what kind of trouble this will cause for the Black Hoods. But seeing as TK and Priest don't seem too worried, I won't worry, either.

Taking a deep breath through my nose, I blow it out slowly through my mouth.

Even after running out on him, he had shown up for me.

He's more than I thought he was. God, he's so much more.

And he's leaving in a couple of days.

Chapter 21

TWATKNOT

CORA GAPES at us when we return. I can't tell if she's happy to see me, or if she's gonna kick me in the junk. Either way, I need answers, so I guess I'll take my chances.

She opens her mouth, about to speak, but I put a finger to her lips and inform her, "You're taking a break now."

Her brown eyes flash with anger as she swats my hand away. "I can't take a break because I have nobody else to work tonight. And besides, if you think you can pull this alpha male bullshit and I'll come running like some stupid little lap dog, you don't know me at all."

Priest waves a hand in my direction and heads around to the far side of the bar. Cora watches him with wide eyes as he walks up and stands next to her.

"There, Priest is on it. Now take. A fucking. Break," I repeat, each syllable laced with increasing frustration.

We compete in a stare down, until finally, Cora's shoulders fall and she turns to Priest, handing him her bottle opener. "I'll be back."

Priest accepts her offering with a smug smirk.

She slips out from behind the bar and I follow, hot on her heels, all the way out the back door and into the alley.

Cora takes a few steps away from me, putting space between us. Space I don't think I can handle. I need to know who that guy is, why he scares her, and why he's harassing her?

And why seeing her anywhere near another man drives me fucking crazy?

I want to kiss her lips and claim her. I want to fuck her against the wall of this bar to show her that she's fucking mine. I want to shake her until she stops glaring at me the way she is right now.

"Who the fuck is he?" I demand.

Cora folds her arms over her chest. "He's none of your concern."

"The fuck he isn't. First, he follows you and your boy, scaring the shit out of you both, and now he's come to harass you at work. Who the fuck is he?" I snarl. "Who is he to you?"

She paces in front of me, her hands fisted in frustration.

"Either you fucking tell me, or I'll hunt that piece of shit down and find out for myself. One way or another, I'll get my answer. You know I will."

Cora stops her pacing and throws her arms up in the air. "Why can't you just leave this alone? This isn't your problem—*I'm* not your problem."

In two strides, I eliminate the distance between us. I keep moving until her back hits the brick wall. "That's where you're wrong, Cora. You're mine. I think we established that earlier today, before you ran out on me."

Cora stares up at me, her eyes filled with anger, as well as desire.

"Who is he?" I ask, my voice softer now, gentler.

Anger and desire turn to shame. Turning her head away, she whispers, "He's Harrison's father."

I take a moment to think that through. *His father. Harrison's father is a biker.* It all clicks into place. This is why she hates the rally so much, why she's so jaded. It's because of him.

"He hurt you," I conclude. "Which means he's the reason your dad threatened me with a fucking spatula not to hurt you."

This makes her laugh. "My dad did what?"

"Not important," I say. "Is he why?"

She leans back against the wall and rests her forehead

against my chest. "Yes," she admits. "Every year, I leave town when bike week comes around, because I never want to risk him finding out about Harrison. But this year, my boss got hurt, and he needed me here."

She raises her head and looks up at me, her eyes filled with unshed tears. "I never should've agreed to take Harrison to see the motorcycles the other day, but he loves them so much. And since this was his first time being here for bike week, I couldn't tell him no." Reaching up, she wipes her eyes with her fingers. "I hate being here for the rally, because it reminds me of what happened."

"What happened?" I ask, placing my finger under her chin so she can't look away. "Tell me everything, Cora."

"A few years ago, I went to a concert with a couple of friends during the rally, and Big Dick was there. We were all drinking, hanging out in one big group. I only had two drinks that night, but they were apparently too many because I blacked out. I woke up a few hours later, naked in a tent, and he was on top of me. My head was so fuzzy, and I could barely move."

I want nothing more than to go out and kill that fucker, but I need to know the rest.

"Did he—" I start, trying to find the strength to ask what I know she's holding back. "Did he rape you?" I hiss through gritted teeth.

A tear slides down her cheek. "I don't even remember

going back to that tent with him. When I woke up, I tried to push him off, but I could barely move my arms, and he had a hand over my mouth, and…" Her voice trails off, like she's seeing it all over again.

The words echo inside of my head. *I tried to push him off… He had a hand over my mouth…*

"I'll fucking kill him," I seethe. "I'm going to kill that fucker for what he did, for you and for Harrison."

Cora grabs my hands and pulls them to her chest. "TK, you can't. For the same reason I never reported it. He's the president of a large, very dangerous MC. They'll kill you and me both."

"He raped you!" I roar, shoving away from the wall. This time, it's me pacing the alley, every muscle in my body tensed with rage. "He deserves a fucking bullet between his eyes for what he did to you."

Her voice is soft now. "But I don't remember what happened. Maybe I could've asked for it."

That stops me in my tracks. "Getting drunk and passing out is not an invitation for sex, Cora. Even if you had offered before that, the second you were unconscious, that invitation was off the fucking table."

"I don't know. I was so fucked up back then, TK. Adrift, I guess."

"That still doesn't make it right, Cora. He violated you."

An internal struggle wages inside of me, and anger

clouds my vision. Killing him would be too merciful for what he'd done to her. He took away a piece of her innocence. His actions had hardened her heart against any man who tried to break through the steel barricade around it. Cora didn't deserve that.

And the worst part of it all is, she feels responsible for his actions. Could I really walk away and just let that son of a bitch live?

The answer is clear—I can't.

"Let me do this for you," I say, moving closer, placing my hands against the wall on either side of her head.

Her eyes are sad as she peers up at me. "No."

"I can't let it go, Cora. Not knowing what I do now. That fucker needs to die."

"Please."

I stare down at her, memorizing the curve of her cheek and the arch of her brow. "He's gonna pay for every ounce of pain he put you through."

"Then you're no better than he is," she declares.

Her words hit me like a bullet, and the air between us changes. Fire roars beneath my skin.

"I'm nothing like him," I growl, my jaw clenched. "I might wear a cut, but that doesn't make me some kind of monster, Cora. Have I done things I'm not proud of? Yes. But I have never robbed a woman of her innocence like he has. Wanting to protect you should be proof enough of that for you."

She places her hands on my chest and shoves me back, breaking the contact between us as fury fills her face. "The only thing it shows me is that I made a mistake coming to that motel room."

I snort. "Stop lying to yourself, Cora. You know there's something between us. You'd never have told me the truth if there wasn't. And what happened with us in that motel..." I shake my head. "You felt that too. I know you did. Why do you think I need to do this? Why do you think I'd risk everything to take out a threat to you and Harrison?"

"If you do this, it just shows you don't respect me or what I want. You want to go down this path? Fine, kill him, but know this... only in a biker's world would this be a conversation between two people. Feelings or no feelings, me and my son won't be associated with that kind of life."

I gape at her, not knowing what to say.

She's right, this isn't a normal conversation. This isn't the way things work in the regular world. But doesn't she understand? Doesn't she know that letting this go means knowing he's still out there, breathing the same air as her, and that I just can't let that happen?

"He's followed you, Cora," I say, the anger in my voice gone. "He's come to the place where you work. What happens if I'm not around to stop him?"

Cora squares her shoulders. "I'll deal with it."

"You shouldn't have to. Let me protect you."

"I have to go back to work."

She tries to maneuver around me, but I stop her, putting myself between her and the door. "You can't go home while he's in town," I reason. "So you're staying with me."

"Like fuck I am. I have a son, remember? A job, my parents."

Taking her hand in mine, I raise it to my lips. "They'll be fine. He doesn't know where you live. You told me that yourself."

"No," she snaps, her voice hard, but I can tell she's wavering.

"Stay with me, Cora, please." I press a kiss to the back of one hand, and then the other. "We'll finish out your shift, get your stuff, and then you and I can go back to the motel just until he's gone."

Cora looks away, her jaw ticking as she thinks.

"I'll respect your wishes, baby, but you've gotta respect mine. Let me keep you and Harrison safe."

When her eyes meet mine again, I know I've won the battle. "Fine," she says with an exaggerated sigh. "But I'm only doing it because you said please."

I smile. If that's all it takes, I'm about to say that word more than I've ever said it before.

CORA

"WHICH BED ARE YOU SLEEPING ON?" I ask as I come out of the bathroom. I'd washed my face, brushed my teeth, put on a nightgown that's admittedly much sexier than the ones I usually wear, and now I just want to go to bed and forget the past few days ever existed.

TK pulls his shirt over his head and shrugs. "Depends. Which one are you sleeping on?"

I point to the one closest to the bathroom, then pull back the blankets and slide under them. My eyes are only closed for a second when I hear the rustle of fabric, then something hit the floor.

He didn't.

I peek through a slit eye and realize that he did. TK had just dropped his pants in the middle of the floor and was stalking toward me in all his naked glory. I'm about to protest, but he moves to the bed I'm in and pulls back the covers on the other side.

"Excuse me! I'm sleeping in this one."

Sliding his legs beneath the blanket, he covers himself up to his waist and turns to face me, propping his head up with his hand, giving me a shit-eating grin. "I know."

My belly dips. "Get out!"

He sticks out his tongue and glides it across his lips while staring down at me. "Kiss me."

Oh, he is exasperating!

"No, TK. Get out of my bed."

"I will if you can kiss me and tell me that you still want me to sleep over there."

I glare at him, my anger only a farce at this point, because my eyes drop to his lips.

They're so full and soft, and I will never forget the way they had felt on every part of my body.

Fucking hell, Cora. Are you really going to do this?

"I really fucking want you to kiss me, Cora. I want to fucking bury myself so deep inside you, we won't know where you start and I end. But after everything I've learned tonight, I need you to make the first move."

I don't have far to go to press my lips to his. Slowly, I lift my head from the pillow and roll onto my side, using my elbow to hold my weight so I can lean up and kiss him.

The instant our lips touch, he smiles against mine. *Fucker.*

Gripping my waist, he pulls me on top of him. I'm leaning over him now, relishing in the way his lips devour me, heart and soul, ripping me out of my body and rocketing me off to a heavenly plane clinging to him, desperate to take him with me.

"Fuck, baby, you're so soft."

Fat, mouthy bartender.

The words swim through my brain in TK's voice, but his hand is slipping the strap of my nightgown down, allowing my breast to fall free from the thin material. He pulls his mouth away and looks down, his thumb coming up to glide over it before looking back up at me.

"You're beautiful."

And I melt. My body, my icy soul, as well as the anger I'd felt at his actions since the day I met him.

His hand cups the back of my neck and he pulls me closer, his lips slow and gentle against mine. His thumb continues to rub across my nipple, and I moan as the sensation sends zings of pleasure rocketing to my core.

The last time we had sex, it'd been hard and fast, but this time is different. He's making a statement, taking his time. And he might not know it, but he's making me fall for him just a little bit more.

Time stands still as we kiss. Our fingers explore each

other's bodies, our hearts beating in tandem inside our heaving chests.

There have been others besides Big Dick, a couple of them even good. But none of them had ever made me feel the way TK feels beneath me right now. His touch feels like worship, and his whispered words are like a prayer.

"Ride me, baby."

Fat, mou —

The memory doesn't even get a chance to play out before he arranges my legs on either side of his hips. "I see you overthinking, Cora. Stop that shit right now." He grinds his hips up, his cock gliding through the wetness between my legs. "You feel that?"

I bite my lip and stare at him, unable to speak.

"That's because I'm fucking crazy about you. And this silky fucking nighty is about to be the goddamn death of me."

I let his words sear into my heart.

"Please," he whispers.

My body quivers with need, and even though it takes some effort, I shove that nasty memory aside.

With one hand between us, I roll on the condom he hands me, and gently settle myself down over his length. The moan that escapes my lips is only drowned out by his.

"Fuck, baby. I feel like you were fucking made for me."

I roll my hips and stare down at him. His cheeks are pink and ruddy, and his nostrils flare as he leans up and kisses me.

Together we move, and I feel him everywhere—under me, inside of me, around me—and still, it's not enough.

"Jonas," I moan.

"Fuck, Cora. I—"

Then suddenly, he's pushing me off of him and sliding down between my legs, putting my pussy just above his face.

I instantly feel insecure. I'm too big for this. I probably weigh as much as he does.

"Grab the headboard, baby."

He licks along my crease to my nub.

"I'm too—"

He sucks my clit between his lips, flicking it wildly with his tongue, causing me to cry out. Not able to hold myself up, I do as he said and grab the headboard.

"Ride my face, Cora." It's an order. I've never seen anything as sexy as him below me, his lips just inches from my aching pussy.

"I'll squish you," I say, totally mortified to admit that.

He squeezes my hips. "Squish me, fucking suffocate

me, and I'll die a happy man. But for the love of God, get out of your head and feed me this sweet pussy."

I gape down at him, and the dare in his eyes is clear.

Gripping the headboard, I toss my head back, rolling and rocking against his mouth. He pants and grunts, and I continue to move, reveling in the feel of his beard on my tender flesh, while his tongue builds the burn between my legs.

When I come apart, he laps up my pleasure like it's the nectar from a peach.

"God, Jonas…" Lights explode behind my eyelids. My heart's beating so fast, I fear it'll gallop right out of my chest.

His tongue disappears, and I'm still catching my breath when he presses soft, gentle kisses along my crease, my clit, and between my inner thighs.

Sliding up from underneath me, he flips me over onto my back in one swift move.

"Now it's my turn."

Cupping my breast, he leans down and laps at my nipple as he thrusts back inside of me.

This time, it's not slow or gentle, which is fine. This is what I want.

He takes me hard and fast, riding me this time. His hips roll in a way I've never seen, filling me, hitting the right spot again and again.

"God, Cora. Fucking perfect."

His hips lose their rhythm, and his body trembles beneath my fingertips. Then, with one deep thrust, he pauses, his length buried deep, tipping us both over the edge.

Minutes pass as we lie there, our breathing ragged, and our skin covered in sweat.

TK presses a tender kiss to my lips. "You can say a lot of things about the two of us, but you can never say what we do to each other is a mistake." He grins. "And I'm sleeping in this fucking bed."

Chapter 23

TWATKNOT

PULLING up to Cora's house, I spy Priest off to the side, lying back in a lawn chair with a beer in his hand. The fucker looks like some bad biker lawn gnome that Cora's parents had installed in their yard out of pity, because he was the last one left at the garden center.

I shake my head and chuckle.

"What's so funny?" Cora asks from behind me.

"Nothing."

I back my bike into the driveway and dismount. Helping Cora off, I stalk toward a smiling Priest, waving at us with the amber bottle in his hand.

"I thought you were supposed to be watching the house."

He peers up at me over the top of his sunglasses. "I am."

"I thought the priest only drank the sacrificial wine?"

"Dude, Cora's dad just keeps giving them to me. It would be rude of me to say no."

I shake my head. "You really are the worst priest in the history of the church."

"Damn right I am." He takes a healthy swallow. "But this priest has a steady supply of beer when I'm on duty at this place, 'cause Cora's old man is cool as hell."

He's not wrong there.

I look over my shoulder for Cora, who's fussing with her hair a few feet away, and ask Priest in a low voice, "Any sign of him?"

"Not a fucking peep. This is a pretty quiet street. There's a nosey old lady across the way that keeps giving me the evil eye from behind the curtains in her front room. I think she likes me."

"I bet she does."

Cora's parents weren't happy to find Priest stationed outside their house in the middle of the night. A frantic phone call and an explanation later, Jim had finally accepted the help I offered, but I knew he'd have some choice words for me sooner rather than later. And sooner just happened to be today, after they insisted we come here for dinner tonight to talk. Or, as Cora had put it, to be interrogated.

Cora comes up from behind me. "You ready for this?"

"Ready as I'll ever be."

We leave Priest to his lawn chair and head inside.

Harrison comes barreling down the hallway, slamming headlong into Cora's legs. She stumbles a bit before finding her balance.

"Momma, I missed you so much," he murmurs against her thighs. She leans down, bringing her little boy into a hug. She kisses the top of his dark hair as he rattles off words so fast, I barely catch half of what he's saying.

"I missed you too, baby. Were you good for Nana and Papaw?"

He scrunches up his face. "They wouldn't let me play outside. Nana said I had to stay in the house."

She gives him a pouty face. "I'm sorry, buddy."

He looks up then and peers at me from over her shoulder. "You're the biker man that helped my momma."

"I am."

"His name is Jonas," Cora tells him, and I have to bite back a smile when Harrison rolls his eyes.

"I know, Mom. He already told me that the first time."

Cora seems taken aback, but Harrison pays her no mind. "Do you have a motorcycle?"

"Absolutely. It's just outside."

Eyes wide, he looks out the front window to get a glimpse of it. "Momma, he has a motorcycle! Did you know that?"

"I did."

He turns his attention to me. "Can I see it, pleeeease?"

"Only if it's okay with your momma."

"Can I see it, Momma? Please?"

His face is lit up like a fucking Christmas tree, and I know that I'm a goner already. The kid has mastered the art of being cute.

At Cora's nod, Harrison squeals, kicking his legs until Cora puts him down. He reaches for my hand, his tiny one fitting into mine with room to spare, then he's tugging me toward the door.

"Let's go!"

I laugh, allowing this little boy to think he's dragging me outside under his own power. Pushing open the screen door, he gasps.

"Momma! It's the bird bike! Is that yours?"

"Yes, it is."

Letting him take the lead, I almost laugh out loud when I see his mouth hanging open and his eyes nearly bugging out of his head.

"What's that?" he asks, pointing to the pipe running along the bottom.

"That's the exhaust pipe."

"And that?"

"The gas tank."

"My momma has a bird on her arm just like that," he

tells me. "And that?" He points toward the back of the bike.

I'm staring at Cora when I tell him, "The fender."

I had noticed her tattoos, and though I've had her naked, I haven't yet had the pleasure of exploring her body, finding every freckle and tracing every tattoo on it. Does she really have a phoenix on her arm? Is her reason the same as mine?

Harrison is testing the word I've said, giggling when he says it. "Fen-der. That's a funny word."

"It sure is."

He peers over his shoulder at his mom, and then back at me. "Can you take me for a ride?"

"Harrison, honey," Cora interjects. "You're too little to go for a ride."

"But Momma, I'm not too little. Please, Mr. Jonas."

"Harrison, I…" Sighing, I go down on one knee, putting us at eye level. "It's up to your mom."

Cora crouches down next to him, and he presses his little body against her knees. He takes her face into his little hands and pleads, "Please, Momma. I won't ask for anything else ever again. I just want to take a ride with Mr. Jonas."

I see the worry in her eyes. Worry I now know the cause of. As much as she wants to keep him away from bikers and motorcycles, his keen interest in both is apparent to even me.

"Can he even ride safely with you?" she asks.

"He can," I say slowly. "I don't have a helmet that'll fit him, but I can take it slow."

She considers this.

"It's entirely up to you. I don't mind."

"Pleeease, Momma," he begs.

After a moment, she relents. "Fine. But only around the block, and no speeding." The second part is aimed at me.

Harrison squeals, dancing around the driveway like a little elf high on too many cookies, singing, "I'm going on a ride! I'm going on a ride!"

Priest chortles from his lawn chair, and I can't hide my own smile. I'm not normally a kid guy, but this kid is the shit.

Throwing my leg over the seat of my motorcycle, Cora lifts Harrison into her arms and hands the wiggling child over to me. He's a tiny little thing, and I easily settle him in front of me, his body nestled securely between my arms. I give him a few quick directions on how to use his legs to squeeze around the gas tank to keep his balance. He laughs when he reaches his little arms out toward the handlebars, but falls short.

I flick the ignition, and his happy laughs are nearly louder than the engine beneath us.

"When we move, I want you to hold on tight with your legs and lean back against me."

"Okay, Mr. Jonas." He grips the sides of my jeans. "Let's go!"

"Please be careful," Cora urges, looking ready to pass out.

"He's safe with me," I promise.

Balancing myself, I pop the kickstand, taking all the weight of the motorcycle on myself. We move forward carefully until I reach the end of the driveway.

"Remember what I told you," I say, my voice raised over the rumble of the engine. Harrison just smiles and nods in reply. "Okay, little man. Here we go."

I take one last glance over at Cora, standing there with her arms wrapped around her body in the driveway. She mouths the words, "be careful," and I tip my chin.

I push forward, twisting the throttle and giving the engine a little gas. We glide onto the street at a glacial pace, allowing Harrison to adjust to the feel. It's not until we get out of Cora's sight that I open it up a little more. Harrison cheers, and I can't contain my own laughter at his genuine happiness. He squirms, but I wrap my left hand around him, securing his frame to my front. It's not easy to drive like this, but I value my life, and Cora would kill me if I let anything happen to this guy.

We make it around one block, and then another. And then I decide to take us around a few more times before returning to Cora's parents' house. As I back us in and kill the engine, Harrison is all laughs and smiles.

"What did you think?" I ask him.

"I want to go again!"

"I bet you do, buddy."

"Mr. Jonas, do you like my momma?" Before I can reply, he adds, "Because I think she likes you a whole lot."

Cora approaches and plucks him off the bike, listening to him jabber away, giving me a moment to allow the heaviness of his question to settle in.

I do like her, little man. I like her a whole fucking lot.

CORA

"OVER THERE," Harrison cries, tugging on my hand and pointing toward a game booth where kids can fish in a kiddie pool and bring up little plastic fish to win a prize. "Can I play?"

Seeing TK watching my son with a smile on his face causes a warm feeling to build inside my chest. A feeling I've been growing accustomed to the past few days.

"Come on, little man." Reaching down, he takes Harrison's free hand. "Let's win your momma a stuffed animal."

I release Harrison, and the pair of them run toward the game booth like a pair of kids, despite the fact that one of them is nearly thirty years old.

I've never given a lot of thought to Harrison not having a father in his life. He's had my father, and men don't get much better than him. But my father isn't his, and as much as my dad has filled a critical role for my son, Harrison has always been aware that he doesn't have an actual dad.

I wrap my arms around myself and smile as TK and Harrison each grab a pole, waving at me before dipping the giant hooks into the water.

"Cora?"

Surprised to hear my name, I turn to see Kenny Slade approaching. As soon as he's in front of me, he pulls me in for an unexpected hug.

"Kenny!" I give him a quick pat on the back before stepping away. "It's been forever. How are you?"

"Almost seven years. And I've been good. I've moved around a lot, and even spent some time over in Africa, helping out with World Vision. Doing the whole humanitarian thing, ya know? Building homes and schools and stuff."

As the surprise of his sneak attack hug fades, my smile turns genuine. Kenny and I had been friends long ago. In fact, there was a time when I'd thought he was my person, the one I would marry.

But Kenny hadn't seemed too interested in a romantic relationship with me back then, and had been so focused on his career and philanthropy. After high school, he'd moved away.

"I just came home to see Mom and Dad," he tells me,

stuffing his hands into his pocket, his eyes scanning me from head to toe. "You look amazing."

What girl doesn't like to hear that from the boy she'd once thought she was in love with?

Feeling my cheeks grow warm, I say, "Thanks. You too."

He takes a step closer. "Listen, I uh… I was actually hoping I would run into you this week. My mom said you were working at the Moose Knuckle, so I was going to stop by there tonight."

I blink, taking a moment to try to understand that. "To see me?"

A pink hue creeps up past the collar of his shirt, right to the tips of his ears. "Uh…" He clears his throat. "Yeah. I, uh… I've kinda been keeping tabs on you. Ya know, like on social media and stuff?"

I don't know how to respond to that, so I just gape at him as he fumbles to explain himself.

"I've always kinda regretted the way we left things. I thought maybe you and I could like, I don't know, go out to dinner or something?"

"My momma's having dinner with me and Jonas," Harrison tells him, marching between us clutching a ridiculously large stuffed armadillo as he glares up at Kenny.

It takes him a moment to recover, but I have to give

Kenny credit when he crouches down to talk to my son. "Hi, I'm Kenny, an old friend of your mom's."

Harrison narrows his eyes, and it's at that moment I feel the tension in the air. A quick glance over my shoulder, I see TK mere inches away, his eyes narrowed at Kenny.

"My momma has enough friends. She doesn't need old ones."

"Harrison," I scold. "Be polite."

"It's all right. I..."

His voice trails off as he takes in the pissed off biker at my back.

Sighing, I turn to the side and wave my hand toward TK. "Kenny, this is TK. TK, this is my friend Kenny."

Neither of them say a word, only barely containing their sneers while managing chin lifts in the other's direction. *Men.*

But I'm glad TK and Harrison had interrupted. It's odd to think about, but years ago, I would have given anything for Kenny to confess he thought about me and cyber-stalked my social media. A dinner date with him would've been a dream come true for high school Cora. But grown-up Cora likes things a little more... manly.

"Thank you for the offer, Kenny," I say, taking Harrison's hand. "I do have plans tonight. But it was so wonderful to see you."

Taking another look at TK, he presses his lips together and nods. "Take care of yourself, Cora."

"You too," I say to his retreating back.

Watching him leave, I marvel at how much things can change in just a few years.

"Who was that?" TK asks, stepping around to face me.

"Just an old friend."

TK's eyes narrow as he watches Kenny disappear into the crowd. "That hug looked super friendly," he points out. His tone is light, but the possessive glint in his eye makes my belly flutter with desire. And that just pisses me off.

"What do you care, anyway?" I snap.

Raising his brows, he tilts his head to the side. "Cora…"

I look down at Harrison, but he's paying us no attention. He's busy deciding which game he can play next to win another stuffed animal.

I take a step closer to TK and lower my voice. "No, seriously, why do you care?" I poke him in the chest, gently at first, then again, this time much harder. "You're leaving in a couple of days, you said so yourself, so what's it to you who I hug?"

Wrapping his hand around mine to keep me from poking him a third time, his eyes grow hard. "You're in my bed, Cora. And when you're in my bed, you don't go hugging other men."

I bark out a laugh, unable to believe my ears. "In the few days I've known you, I've seen you with three blondes and two different brunettes, and you were doing a hell of a lot more than hugging."

"That was before," he counters, giving my hand a gentle squeeze.

I'm not buying it. "Why are you here?"

He releases my hand, but doesn't step away. "What the fuck are you talking about?"

"You," I say, unable to hold it in another second. "Me. Why are you here after everyone left?"

He looks down at my son. "Not here, Cora. This isn't the time nor the place."

But now that I've unleashed the question, I can't stop myself. "I mean it! What are you really here for? Since when does the hot biker stick around to protect the fat, mouthy bartender?"

Rage flashes in his eyes, and he pulls me close, putting his lips at my ear. His heart's thumping so hard against his chest, I can feel it against mine. "No more, Cora," he hisses, his anger barely under control. "I have apologized for those words over and over again. I've even sung you a song, for fuck's sake. I beat myself up over that shit every damn day, so either you get over it or you don't, but you can't keep throwing that in my face every time you start to feel something for me."

"Momma?"

I can't tear my eyes away from his. The passion and the anger and the regret are all there, plain as day, waiting for me to accept his apology once and for all, and allow us to move on.

"Momma?"

"Just a second, baby."

"I can admit when I'm wrong, Cora," TK continues, "but I'm not going to knock myself out apologizing for something you're never going to forgive."

God, he's right.

I'm still holding a grudge, and for whatever reason, that problem is mine. He's apologized and tried to make amends. Me holding onto my anger just shows that I'm more broken than I would ever want to admit.

"I forgive you."

I melt just a little when he cups the side of my face. "You're beautiful, Cora. And no, I don't own you, you're not my possession, but I'm starting to think that maybe I'm yours."

And that's the moment I realize I might actually be falling in love with this man.

Chapter 25

TWATKNOT

SINCE THE NIGHT Priest and I tossed Big Dick out of the bar, there's been no sign of him or his club snooping around. I'd even put out feelers with a few of the locals I'd met at the Moose Knuckle, but those had come back with nothing as well. If the guy is still here, he's hiding, and likely planning something. And if he is, the danger to Cora and Harrison is still out there.

Cora insisted that she has to keep working, though, claiming her boss needs her, which annoys the ever-loving fuck out of me. But whether I said yes or no, she'd still be here. If I've learned anything about this woman, it's that she's her own person, and defiantly stubborn to the fucking core. So, here I sit, bellied up to the bar, watching her work tonight while Priest keeps an eye on the house. Most of the biker crowd has thinned out with the rally finishing up.

There are still some tourists around, but here at the Moose Knuckle, it's mostly locals in attendance tonight.

"You want another one of your pussy drinks?" Cora asks, grinning.

"No, ma'am," I reply. "Got a hot date later. I need to be sober to get us back to my motel." I have things planned for her tonight, and those plans have my cock straining against the fly of my jeans. Though Cora would never admit it aloud, she likes staying in my room as much as I like her being there.

"Someone I know?"

"Nah. This girl's a local. Long brown hair, nice set of tits." I lean forward. "And I think she likes me."

Cora's eyes grow wide, but she recovers quickly, her lips quirking up in a half-smile. "And what about you? Do you like her too?

I reach out and pluck a lock of hair from her breast, letting my hand linger when I graze her nipple. "Oh, I like her a lot," I confess.

"Lucky girl," she breathes.

Fuck me, she's beautiful.

"I'll be sure to tell her when I have my head between her thighs tonight." The old man next to me chokes on his beer, and Cora stifles a gasp, her eyes wide with shock.

A gorgeous blush creeps across her cheeks. Pulling

her hair from my hand, she admonishes playfully, "I'm at work."

"Get the other bartender to help out, we can sneak to the back."

"Not happenin', mister. Besides, I already rubbed one out in the shower."

It's my turn to gape at her. The old man is definitely still listening. His eyes are on the beer in front of him, but his body is leaning toward us to hear better, but I don't care. I think of Cora, shiny and wet in the shower, rivulets of soap suds dripping from her nipples, her fingers slipping between her legs and her lips parted wide…

Fucking hell.

My jeans grow tighter, if that's possible, and I look away, trying to think of anything but her sweet moan as she came before we got here.

Knowing damn well she's won the battle, she strides off to help a customer.

As she works away, my phone pings with an incoming text from Priest, giving me a status update.

All clear.

Good. Almost done here, then back to the motel.

Three little dots pop up on the screen.

Wear a condom.

Rolling my eyes, I send him the middle finger emoji, then watch the little dots bounce, waiting for his reply.

Call Hashtag. Maybe he can get some information on this fucker so I don't have to keep sweating my balls off in this damn lawn chair.

I highly doubt Cora's mother would ever let him sweat to death. Yesterday, during my watch of the house, she'd brought me a never-ending supply of cold drinks, as well as a fan attached to a little orange extension cord. Priest's likely living it up tonight on guard duty, but he's right. We can't stand sentry outside her house forever. As long as that douchebag is out there, Cora and her family are in danger. We have to come up with a more permanent solution.

I catch Cora's eye and point to an empty section of the bar. "Gonna go make a phone call."

Nodding, she resumes filling the fridge that runs along the back counter.

Making my way to the empty space, I lean my ass against a table while pulling up Hashtag in my contacts. If anyone can find information on Big Dick, it's that smart son of a bitch.

The phone rings twice before he answers.

"Whatever it is you want, the answer is no," he growls into the phone. I hear a commotion in the background... kids yelling, adults yelling...

"The fuck's goin' on there?"

Hashtag groans in frustration. "Dude, you don't wanna know."

"It's not fair!" someone shouts from the other end of the line. *Interesting.*

"Oh," I drawl, "I think I do."

"Let's just say that GP's in deep shit."

Okay, now that's surprising. GP's usually the perfect one, which is part of the reason Judge had entrusted him and his old lady to watch the kids while we were here. "You're going to have to give me more than that, man."

Hashtag's voice is without any humor when he says, "Let's just say GP wasn't watching the kids as closely as we thought."

"Oh, fuck." I bark out a laugh. "Your daughter?"

"Yup," he answers dryly.

"And…"

"Kevin."

I lose it then, unable to stop myself. Cora and a few others glance over in my direction, but I wave them off.

"It's not funny, TK," Hashtag mutters. "Shelby's on the warpath, and Judge is considering a chastity belt for the both of them."

I try to calm my laughter and keep my voice even. "And how are you handling it?"

"I want to kill the fucking kid," he grouses. "But I think Judge has that part under control."

Hashtag and Shelby's daughter has been getting pretty close to Judge's adopted son, but they're young.

As funny as it is that they got caught, one part does put me on edge. "Did they…?"

"Fuck no, and they won't ever, not until long after I'm dead."

"You were probably doing worse than that when you were their age," I remind him.

"When you have kids of your own, you can give me advice, asshole," he retorts. "Now, how about you tell me why you called so I can get back out there and play referee."

"I need you to do some of your computer shit and get me some info."

Hashtag's voice changes, turning all business. "Why?"

I watch Cora smile at one of her customers and tell him, "As a favor to a friend."

"Would this friend be the mouthy bartender that came for breakfast the other day?"

"What if it is?"

Hashtag laughs. "Relax, TK. Last time I checked, you were old enough to have an old lady."

I'm going to kill that gossiping fucking boy scout. An old lady? Is that what Cora is to me? Is that what I want? Is that what she wants?

I close my eyes and sigh. I can figure all that shit out later. "I need you to check out the Screwballs MC."

"Shouldn't be too hard," he assures. "And here I

thought you were going to ask me to hack into some clinic and have your STD results changed or something. What should I be looking for?"

"The usual—locations, members, any issues with the law."

"Should be a cake walk, but I have to ask. Does this have anything to do with that asshole who was following Cora that day?"

I struggle not to tell him about the connection of that club to Cora, or Harrison's origins. None of it would help him find the information I need, but it would provide a driver to getting it quickly... No, it's her story to tell. I won't violate her trust like that.

"It does," is all I give him.

Knowing he's curious, he doesn't push. "Yeah, sure, man. Might take me a few hours, though."

"That's fine. Anything you find will be helpful."

"Is she in trouble or something?" he asks. "If she is, I'm sure Judge might consider letting you stay longer."

My heart nearly stops. "Wait, what?"

"Didn't Priest tell you? Judge wants you and Priest home as soon as possible."

A pang of dread punches me in the gut. Judge wants us home, back in Austin. I've known all along that I have to go back. I just put it out of my mind for a bit. Austin is my home, but for an unexplainable reason, going back seems almost foreign.

"He didn't relay that to me," I say after a moment. "How soon is soon?"

"Judge didn't specify, but you know him. Soon means yesterday."

"I see."

Commotion rings loudly through the receiver. Hashtag yells out something, and Shelby's angry voice nearly shatters my eardrum.

"Hey, man, I gotta run. I'll text you what I find."

"Sounds good. Have fun, man."

The connection goes dead, but all I can do is stare at my phone, thinking of what I have to do.

How do I tell Cora I have to go back?

CORA

"I DON'T REMEMBER the last time I've been on a date," I admit, smiling across the table at TK.

"I've never been on one in my life," he replies.

"What?" My voice echoes through the restaurant. Everyone stops what they're doing and turns to look at us. Forcing a smile, I wave an apology before leaning forward and lowering my voice. "What? How have you *never* been on a date?"

TK shrugs. "Just never met anyone I wanted to actually spend time with."

Leaning back in my seat, I take a sip of my wine and consider that. "Never?"

"Nope."

"Then why me?" The question is out before I can stop it, and part of me regrets saying it out loud because it shows a weakness in me. But the other part of me is desperate to hear his answer.

"You're not just anyone. You're special."

His line is so cheesy, but even after everything that's happened between us, I'm begging to believe him. What other reason would this man have for sticking around Sturgis when the motorcycle rally is packed up and gone? What other man would stick his neck out against the president of a motorcycle club for a single mother he wasn't interested in?

"You like me."

He raises his brow. "I guess you could say that."

"You do. You like me."

"Well, you like me too," he replies, grinning.

"Sometimes I do."

TK barks out a laugh. "Fuckin' liar."

I grin at him in response at the same time the waitress returns to our table with our drinks and a basket of bread.

Silence fills the space between us as we sample the warm bread and our drinks.

"Why do you have a phoenix on your motorcycle?" I ask.

He considers my question before responding. "My old man is the pastor of a church up in New York State." He stares down at the table, and I can tell instantly this is something he's not used to talking about.

"Most people would think my childhood was perfect, with my dad running the church and my mom being a homemaker, doing whatever the hell he told her to." Anger drips from those last few words. "I did too, for a long time. I went to school, said my prayers, collected bibles and pamphlets from the church pews after each service." His eyes dance when he looks up at me. "I was a literal choir boy."

That makes me smile. "Whoa, that couldn't have been good. I've heard you sing."

Chuckling quietly, he shakes his head. "Dad wanted me to go to some stuck-up bible college in Upstate New York, and I did, just because I didn't want to upset the old man, ya know? But everything I did upset him, always. Even when I was a kid, my parents disapproved of my friends, my taste in music, my choice in television shows or sports. Nothing I ever did made them happy."

"I hate that for you." And I do.

"I did it for years," he says, rubbing his chin. "Anyway, bible college wasn't for me, and what I really wanted to do was to learn how to do custom paint jobs. You know, like on motorcycles and cars and shit? Well, no son of my father's was gonna work in a garage. I found a place near the college that was taking on an apprentice, so I applied and got the job."

My jaw clenches, believing I know where this is heading.

"My parents came for a visit, and I was so tired of lying to them, I told them where I'd been working, and they were pissed. My father called me a disappointment, and my mother informed me that she didn't even know who she'd raised. I was broken."

"So, what did you do?" I ask, my heart aching for his younger self.

"I came here for the rally and met a few guys." His lip quirks up in a grin. "One of those guys was Karma. He introduced me to the Black Hoods, and I've been with them ever since."

"And the phoenix?"

"Rebirth. I'm not the same person my parents raised. I'm my own person, and I've made a good life for myself despite them and their religious bigotry. That phoenix is me rising from the ashes of my old life with them."

I like that.

He tips his head toward my arm. "What about your phoenix?"

"Same thing. I got it to represent becoming a new person after having Harrison, and the flames represent my desire to protect him and give him the best life."

"That's quite a coincidence, don't you think?"

I smile. *Coincidence indeed.*

TK and I have been alone together plenty these past few weeks, but in those times, we'd either been fighting or screwing. And now that we're sitting here like civilized adults in a nice restaurant, it's easy to see myself spending more time with him like this.

"You're different," I note.

He pauses with his drink to his lips. "Meaning?"

Shit, Cora. Must you always blurt shit out like that?

"When you're out in public with your club, you're different from when you're here with me, one-on-one."

"I like when I'm with you one-on-one, especially in the motel room."

That's so TK, only concentrating on one part of that sentence. *Such a perv.*

"When I first met you," I continue, attempting to emphasize my point, "you were always so loud and bold, almost like you were putting on a show, entertaining people. But now, like this, you just seem to be yourself."

He considers that. "I guess with you, I can be myself."

"But I thought you guys all think of yourselves as brothers? Are you saying you can't be yourself around them?"

"It's just always been that way. I'm the funny one." The waitress approaches with our steaming plates balanced on a tray. Once she places our food on the table, he waits until she's gone and adds, "I'm also the good-looking one."

"I hate to break it to ya, sweetie, but you're not the only good-looking one," I tease.

"The fuck you say?"

It takes effort, but I'm able to suppress my smile. "All the guys are good looking. Even Judge is hot, and he's old. He's like a sexy silver werewolf or something."

His frown grows, like he just can't see it. "You think Judge is hotter than me?"

I finish chewing my pasta and reveal, "Priest is pretty hot too."

"Priest's a fucking pussy."

"Priest is probably the hottest one out of all of you."

At first, he looks shocked, but that disappears quickly and he smiles. "You're kind of an asshole, Cora. Did you know that?"

"Sure did."

"Perfect. So I'm the hot one and you're the asshole."

"I'd say we're a match."

TWATKNOT

I HELP her into her leather jacket, appreciating how it hugs her curves. It looks good on her.

My patch would look even better.

The thought escapes before I can rein it in. Even I know there's not a snowball's chance in hell that she would be ready for that conversation. I don't even know if *I'm* ready for that conversation, seeing as we're barely even an *us* at this point. And once I tell her that Judge has called me back home, I have no idea where we'll stand.

You need to man up and tell her, asshole.

Guilt has been eating away at me for not telling her yet. And with tonight going so perfectly, my guilt has grown into an aching pain, gnawing away at my insides.

"What did you think?" she asks.

"It was good." The brewery she'd suggested had an

awesome atmosphere, and even better beer. Normally, I wouldn't be a huge fan of the local craft shit, but those guys know their beer as well as their food. "Best damn steak I've had in a long time."

"Aren't you glad we didn't go to that roadhouse you wanted to try?"

"Yeah, yeah, yeah," I mutter, nudging her with my shoulder.

She straightens her jacket and catches me staring. "What?"

"Can't a man stare at a beautiful woman?"

"Did one come in?" she teases, looking behind her.

Stepping forward, I thread my fingers through her long, dark hair and kiss her. Her hands grip my biceps as I pull her closer, deepening the kiss.

Someone behind us clears their throat.

Shit. I'd been so lost in her, I'd almost forgotten that we're standing in the middle of the restaurant with a very engrossed audience.

Cora pulls away first, a familiar blush of pink rising on her cheeks as she bites down on her swollen lip. "We should go."

"We should." My voice is hoarse, and deeper than usual. Before I step away, I press my lips to her ear and whisper, "I'm going to fuck you in nothing but this leather jacket and those fucking heels."

The pink in her cheeks flame to a fiery red, making me feel quite proud of myself for flustering her.

Throwing my arms around her shoulders, I lead her out the doors and toward the parking lot. My mind is swirling with all the filthy things I have planned for her once we get back to the motel. Delicious things that would have her pissing off all of the neighbors when she comes around my cock.

Cora suddenly stops dead in her tracks, pulling me to a halt.

I barely have time to register her reaction when I see a motherfucker with a death wish sitting astride my bike.

Big Dick, President of the Screwballs MC, South Dakota chapter.

"Have a nice date?" he asks, baring his teeth in a nasty grin. Cora's arm trembles around my waist, and I want to reassure her that it's going to be okay, but I'm not taking my eyes off this motherfucker.

"Get off my fucking bike," I tell him, my voice wavering with barely harnessed rage.

Big Dick grins like the Cheshire cat. "See, here's the thing, pretty boy. I've decided that if you can ride the mother of my son, then I can ride your bike. Only seems fair, doesn't it, Cora?"

Strike one, fuckface.

"Don't even look at her," I growl.

My anger is pulsing through me like a living thing,

but Cora presses a hand against my chest, grounding me just enough to keep me from killing this fucker, and reminding me of the promise I had made to her.

"Look, asshole, I'm on a date, and I'm trying really fucking hard to be a nice guy here, but you have two fucking seconds to get off my ride."

"And you'll do what, exactly? I have a right to get to know my only son." The misogynistic bastard. I have a feeling that if Harrison had been a girl, Big Dick wouldn't have given two shits about the kid.

"You will never meet *my* son," Cora spits.

"He's my fucking son too, bitch," he snarls, sliding off my bike and planting his feet on the pavement. His eyes are rimmed red, filled with ire. "If you think I'll let this bastard step into my shoes, you're mistaken."

He moves around the motorcycle, each step bringing him closer. Putting some distance between us and him, I attempt to move Cora behind me, but she shoves her way back to my side, her chin raised in defiance.

"I wouldn't take another step if I were you," I warn, but he ignores me and takes two large steps forward.

Strike two.

"I want my fucking son. He deserves more than just a fat cunt for a mother."

Strike fucking three.

I charge him, my rage taking over all common sense and reason. He had hurt Cora, defiled her body, then discarded her like fucking trash. Now, because she'd given birth to a boy, raised him despite his origins, and given him a good life, this asshole thinks he can walk in here and stake his claim? He'll never see Harrison, I guarantee it.

And that's one promise I intend to keep.

I go in low and slam my shoulder into his gut, sending us both tumbling to the ground. He pushes and shoves, anything to get me away from his flank. He rears forward, fist clenched, and connects with my jaw, forcing my head back from the blow. It hurts like hell and my head swims, but I shove that shit down.

This fucker has to pay for everything he took from Cora and what he wants to take again.

I raise my fist and slam it into his face once, twice, three times.

Big Dick falls back, his head slamming onto the pavement, his arm coming up to block my blows, but I don't let that stop me. I crawl over him, my weight pressing him into the ground as I pummel my fists into his face and head.

Cora's yelling behind me, but I can't make out what she's saying. Blind rage fuels each blow, one right after another, until his face is nearly unrecognizable. *He has to pay. He has to pay.* A mantra that repeats itself in my head with each strike.

Hands tug at my waist, a voice crying behind me. It all seems so far away. "Stop, TK. Please, stop."

Big Dick isn't fighting back anymore.

"You're killing him," the voice sobs.

Good. I want to kill him. His death would end it all and protect her, protect Harrison. It's the only way to stop him from hurting her or anyone else.

"Don't do this. You have to stop." Another hard tug knocks me off balance, and I land beside the bloody mess of a man. He moans, with no real words coming out of his mouth, thanks to the broken jaw I'd given him. Raising my hands, I take in the cuts, gravel, and blood coating them. Then a second pair of hands joins them, smaller ones... Cora's.

"Baby, please stop," she whispers, cradling my face in her hands, those beautiful brown eyes pleading, shining with her tears. "Come back to me," she pleads.

When I lean into her hands, she sighs in relief and presses her lips to my temple, putting her claim on me, or trying to get me back to my senses. Whichever it is, I don't know, nor do I care. All that matters is that she's here, and he's an inch away from death. I only have to finish the job.

"I need to finish this," I tell her.

"No, baby, you did enough."

Baby. That word again. I should relish in it, cherish it, but I'm not done yet.

Her eyes are studying me, trying to figure out what I'm going to do.

"Cora, it's the only way."

"It's not," she says, her face suddenly fierce with determination. "You've won, TK. Look at him."

I peer over at Big Dick. His ragged breaths rattle in his chest, his face covered in blood already swelling. I move then, shifting my body to my hands and knees so that I can lean over his beaten face.

"If you ever come near her or that boy again, I'll end you. You owe her your life, fuck face. The only reason you're still breathing is because of her." I turn and point at Cora. "Breathe in her direction, you die."

His moans are his only response.

Pushing to her feet, she reaches out a hand to me and I grab it, pulling myself up off the ground, and embrace her.

Cora's face rests against my chest. "Let's go home, baby."

She leads me to my motorcycle, and together, we ride away, leaving that son of a bitch to his fate in that parking lot.

CORA

"FUCK, CORA," he hisses, his tattered knuckles moving my hair aside so he can get a better look at his cock between my lips. "Yes, just like that."

Swirling my tongue around the tip, I take him all the way into my mouth until I feel him hit the back of my throat. I gag, swallowing, enjoying the way his body trembles, and seeing his hands clutch the bed sheets.

"I'm gonna come, baby," he growls, his voice deep.

I move faster, taking him deeper while fondling his balls.

His release hits him, and I gladly accept his offering, making a show of swallowing and swirling my tongue around him, slurping up the little bit I'd left behind.

"Jesus Christ, Cora. I've never had my dick sucked like that in my life." His shoulders heave as he stares up at the ceiling.

"You taste good," I purr, dragging my lips along his torso. Flopping onto my back beside him, I nestle my body in the crook of his arm, resting my head on his chest.

"You should teach fucking classes then, because I can't even feel my fucking toes right now."

I laugh softly, drawing lazy circles along the center of his six-pack with the tip of my finger.

"I have something to tell you," he says, running his fingers through my hair. "I've been dreading telling you, but every moment we spend together, I just want to lose myself in you and not the shitty stuff."

I prop my head up on my hand. "Shitty stuff?"

He studies me, his mouth pressed into a thin line. Worry fills my heart as I watch him struggle for the words. "I have to go home tomorrow," he blurts out.

My happy heart plummets back to reality in an instant. Lifting my hand away from his abs, I push myself up into a sitting position beside him. "Like, home to Texas?"

He nods.

I knew this would happen. Hell, I watch this kind of shit happen to other locals every single year during the motorcycle rally, but nothing could have prepared me for the raw ache of it happening to me.

He places my hand against his chest. "I want you to come with me."

"To Texas?" I know it's a stupid question, but so was his.

His expression is serious as he studies me. "Yes. We have something, Cora. Something I didn't even know I wanted, and I don't want to lose that, or you, or Harrison."

Pulling my hand away, I jump out of the bed. "I can't. I can't move to Texas, TK. Are you nuts? My family is here, my *life* is here."

He looks stricken, and I hate that I put that look there, but it can't be helped.

"My life is there," he says.

I stare at him, my head spinning with so many thoughts and emotions. What had I gotten myself into? And Harrison? Oh, God. I'd allowed Harrison to get involved with TK too, and now he's leaving.

How had I gone from being insulted by this man to being rescued by him? Then watching him nearly beat a man to death in my honor, to him making love to me with such tenderness?

"I shouldn't have done this," I say, reaching for my panties. "I knew I shouldn't have done this with you, because I knew it would end like this."

"Cora." TK scrambles out of the bed as I rush around the room, finding my clothes and tugging them on as fast as I can.

"How did I ever think this was a good idea?" I ask,

tugging my shirt down over my head and grabbing my purse off the table near the door. I'm trying so hard to keep myself together as my heart squeezes in my chest.

"Cora, listen." He reaches out and pulls me against his naked body. "This can work. We just have to figure it out."

But he's wrong. There's no way a long-distance relationship would ever work for either of us, especially living different lives.

Popping up on my toes, I press my lips to his stubbled jawline and inhale deeply, memorizing the way he smells. "Thank you for taking care of Big Dick, and for being so good to Harrison."

"Cora."

"Goodbye, TK."

He releases me without a fight. Opening the door, I walk out of the room and down the hall without looking back, and it's not until I get outside that I realize I don't have a car here, and that my house is almost three miles away.

Fuck it, I'll walk.

The roads are empty as I trudge along the sidewalk, thankful for the peace that comes in the middle of the night. As I walk, I replay every encounter I've ever had with TK over and over again in my mind.

If someone would've told me two weeks ago that I'd be walking home, broken-hearted over a biker, I would've laughed my fool ass off. But here I am, alone, sad, and doing just that at three o'clock in the morning.

It never would've worked. I couldn't leave Mom and Dad, and Harrison would be devastated. I also have my job at the bar, and Carl needs me.

My reasons seem less and less plausible with every step I take. Mom and Dad would probably be thrilled to finally get us out of their house, and Harrison would probably just love the adventure.

And do you really want to work for Carl at the Moose Knuckle for the rest of your life?

Ridiculous reasons or not, Sturgis is my home. I mean, could I really give that up for TK, especially so soon? What if…

My head swirls with scenarios and arguments, and by the time I step inside of my parents' home, I can barely keep my eyes open.

What I need is a good night's sleep and a heart to heart with my mother. Not to mention a hug from my sweet boy.

When my head hits the pillow, I can still smell TK on my clothes and my skin. That smell is the only thing that allows my mind to relax and fall into a restless slumber.

TWATKNOT

WE'RE LEAVING Sturgis without Cora and Harrison.

Loading the last of my stuff into my saddlebags, I lean against my bike and look down at my phone, at all the texts I'd sent to Cora last night and this morning. They went unanswered. She'd made her choice last night, and I had to respect that, even if it meant leaving her and Harrison behind. I fucking hate it.

The only consolation to the gaping hole in my heart is that I'm leaving with the threat to them gone. A bystander had found Big Dick after we'd left him there, and if the news was to be believed, he was airlifted out to Sioux Falls, hours away from here and from her. Safe at last.

At least I was able to keep the promise I'd made to protect her.

Priest comes sidling out of the motel's back door with

his pack slung over his shoulder, humming some obnox-
ious tune. He's irritating me already, and we haven't
even left yet.

"You look like shit."

"Go fuck yourself," I growl.

Priest side-eyes me. "Well, aren't you a barrel of
fucking sunshine this morning? This is going to be one
long fucking ride back to Austin," he grouses. "I half-
expected you to walk out here with her on the back of
your bike and the kid in a sidecar. I guess she's not
coming, is she?"

My jaw hardens. I know he means well, but sometimes the man needs to learn when to shut the fuck up.
"They're not."

Priest places his pack onto the back of his bike and
ties it down with a bungee strap. "You know you can
stay. Judge would understand."

Would he, though? His call was clear. Both of us were
needed back in Austin.

The idea of leaving the Austin chapter and going
nomad had played in my mind all night long. Hell, I
hadn't slept a wink just thinking about it. I'd have no
club affiliation, no home chapter to rely on. I'd be on my
own—a lone wolf.

But I'd have Cora and Harrison.

The club's numbers were still down. As the mother
chapter of the Black Hoods, we're weak without new

members. Patching V and Priest had helped, but if shit were to go south again soon, we'd be at a disadvantage, especially if the Screwballs came calling for what I'd just done to one of their presidents.

And I had yet to mention that to Judge or Priest.

"Go see her before we leave," he suggests.

"No. She made her choice."

Fucking hell. I've never felt pain before like I did when I watched her walk out of my room last night. I should've gone after her, convinced her to come with me, but I couldn't. She has a life here. And besides, she didn't want a biker's life anyway, and it's no life for a kid. I just have to come to terms with that, despite the way I feel about her.

I'm not who she needs to be happy.

"It doesn't matter. Are you ready to go?"

"If that's what you want, man, I'm ready."

"Good."

Swinging my leg over my bike, I flick the ignition switch and pop the kickstand. I go to look back, but stop myself before I do. Looking back is only going to hurt more, so I push off and pull out onto the street with Priest trying to catch up.

The white lines of the road flow by. Long, short, long, short. They all blur together.

The asphalt bumps beneath the wheels like a child's lullaby, and no matter how hard I try, my mind keeps drifting back to Cora and Harrison. I think about all the memories I'd made with them these past couple of weeks, and each one stabs me just a little deeper in the chest. My heart aches more the farther we ride from Sturgis, the distance between us growing, separating us forever.

Go back for her.

No, I can't. She doesn't want this life. That's been clear enough all along. She doesn't want me, despite how much I love her and Harrison.

Shock recoils in my system. I *love* her. *I fucking love Cora.*

The realization hits me like a ton of bricks, sending my heart rate pounding out of control. She made her choice, but I didn't. I didn't tell her how I feel. She doesn't even know.

I have to tell her.

The implications of going back lay heavy on my mind, but all I can see is her, our life together. The fucking happily ever after that all my brothers seem to have found. I want that—I *need* that with Cora and Harrison. If going nomad is what it takes, I'll do it, so long as I have them. The rest I'll figure out later.

I have to go back to her. I'll regret it if I don't try.

I signal to Priest and pull off to the side of the road. He kills the engine on his bike, and the fucker is smiling at me.

"You're going back, aren't you?"

"I am."

"Good. That woman and kid—" he peers back over his shoulder toward Sturgis, already fading into the distance, "—they're your home now."

"Now you impart that wise advice on me, *Father*?"

"What can I say? I was a shit priest, though you knew that."

"I do. It's part of the reason why l like you."

"Don't go gettin' all soft on me now, TK."

"You good to go on your own?"

He smiles. "Yeah. Might take the scenic route home, seeing as I haven't seen much of this part of the country. Think I'll take it nice and slow, delay Judge's ass kicking for leaving you here."

"I'll call him and explain why."

"I know you will. He'll be pissed, but he'll understand or he won't. The decision is yours, not his."

I extend my hand out to him and he accepts, gripping it tightly. "Be safe, brother."

"You too." He releases my hand and starts up his bike. "Go get your girl."

My girl. My Cora.

I'm coming home, gorgeous.

Priest takes off, and I turn around, heading back toward town, ignoring the speed limit. There's nothing that'll keep me from her again.

I only make it a few miles when a car comes flying toward me, dust kicking up behind it as it draws closer. The horn honks frantically, but it's only when the car gets close enough that my heart soars.

My Cora, coming after me.

CORA

TK'S HAIR is flying in the wind, making no question as to who's piloting the oncoming motorcycle. I press on the horn again and again, desperate to get his attention.

My car zips right past him and I slam on the brakes, quickly putting my little car in reverse and flying backward to where he's just pulling off to the side of the road.

TK climbs off his motorcycle as I jam the gearshift into park, whip open the door, and attempt to climb out. *Fucking seatbelt.*

Fumbling with the buckle until I'm finally free, I jump out and rush into TK's arms.

"Oh, thank God," I cry, letting the tears spill down my cheeks. "I was so worried I was going to miss you."

TK doesn't say a word, he just wraps his arms around me, burying his face in my neck.

Pressing my lips to the side of his head, I squeeze him tighter, reveling in the feel of being in his arms.

When I'd arrived at the motel and found that both Priest and TK were already gone, my heart sank. But one phone call to my mother was all the encouragement I needed.

Cora, for the love of God, child, go get that man and tell him you love him, or you'll regret it for the rest of your life.

"I love you," I blurt out.

That hadn't exactly been the way I'd planned to tell him, but now that he's here, holding me to him like he'll never let me go, I know that there's no better time than this to just let it all out.

TK pulls back and stares into my eyes. "Fuck, Cora, I love you too, so goddamn much."

I start to laugh, my heart filled with utter joy, when he leans in and kisses the smile right off my lips. So lost in him, I cling to his body, wrapping my legs around his waist as he devours my mouth like a starving man.

Pressing my back up against the side of my car, his hands under my ass, he grinds against me, murmuring, "Fuck, baby."

Reaching down between us, I undo his jeans and breathe against his lips, "I'll go with you," as I release his cock and stroke it in my hand.

"Cora," he pleads, his voice so thick with need, it doesn't sound human.

Moving my flowy shorts to the side, I line his cock at my entrance. Taking that as his cue, he thrusts deep and hard, forcing a gasp from my lungs.

"God, you feel so good," he moans, again plunging deep with one hand on my ass, and the other gripping the roof of the car. "Your fucking pussy was made for me...like fucking velvet."

I can't even speak. All I can do is try to breathe and hold on to his shoulders while he claims me right here on the side of the road.

"Tell me again," he pants, his thrusts growing unsteady.

Squeezing my pussy tight, I glide my tongue across his bottom lip. "I love you, Jonas."

His eyes roll back in his head, and I barely notice a car zooming by because he slams his hips up, his cock coming to a rest as far as it can go. I can feel him pulsating inside of me with his release.

"Fucking right you do," he says once his body has stilled. "Now it's your turn."

I frown, unsure of what he means. Setting me on my feet, he turns me around and presses my front to the car before sliding his hand into my wet shorts.

His fingertip seeks out my swollen nub like a heat-seeking missile and rolls over it once before adding a second finger.

Another car zips by. I know we'll have to hurry if we

want to do this. It's almost seven thirty in the morning, and if we're not finished soon, the commuters will surely get an eyeful.

"Ride my fingers, Cora. Ignore the cars. It's just you and me here."

His hand comes up and wraps around the front of my throat. The act has me groaning and rolling my hips. He tilts my head to the side, his tongue and teeth and lips nipping at the side of my neck while his fingers slide into me.

"Do you love me, Cora?"

"Mhmm."

"Do you understand how fucking much I love you?"

I moan again, but don't answer his question. His grip on my throat tightens, and his teeth sink into my neck just enough to sting. It feels fucking incredible.

"Do you understand how much I fucking love you, Cora?" he asks again, this time annunciating every single word.

The heat between my legs is building to the point of no return. "Yes," I gasp, rolling my hips faster. Reaching down, I cover his hand with mine, forcing his fingers deeper, needing them to end this beautiful ache.

Another car drives by, and then another, and another, but I stay focused on what he's doing, needing my release. He pumps his fingers in and out, and my climax finally rips through me, the force causing me to tremble in TK's arms. His fingers continue to move between my legs, his lips pressed against my ear, telling me I'm beautiful and that he loves me, and that he wants to know what it's like to bury himself inside of me every single morning for the rest of his life.

Finally, completely sated, and a little dazed, I turn in his arms and pull his head down for a sweet, gentle kiss. "I don't know how this is going to work, TK, but I need you."

The grin that spreads across his face will live in my mind forever as one of my most favorite memories.

"I'm yours, baby. For as long as you'll have me, I'm fucking yours."

Chapter 31

TWATKNOT

"COME BACK TO BED," she beckons, her voice thick with desire. She's lying on the bed in my motel room, her face lit up with happiness and a satisfied smile. If only our neighbors had appreciated our reunion last night. The pounding on the wall, and the visit from the concierge for a noise complaint, had been an interesting twist to our evening. Cora was embarrassed as hell, but I reveled in knowing that everyone around heard us. *Jealous bastards.*

"I'll be right back," I tell her, kissing her forehead. "Get some sleep, 'cause I'm not through with you yet."

She giggles. "I thought you'd be tired after last night."

"I don't think I'll ever get tired of you, darlin'." I kiss her lips. "Get some sleep. I won't be long." Rolling out of bed, I grab my phone from the nightstand and step out onto the balcony. I have to call him. The missed calls and texts I'd ignored yesterday are only going to add more fuel to the fire when I knew damn well that Priest had likely already called and checked in on his ride back. Nevertheless, Judge deserves an explanation.

I make the call, and he answers on the first ring like he's been expecting me.

"You better be calling me to tell me you're on the road, TK."

"Right to the fucking point, as always, Judge. Not even a 'Hello, TK. Long time, no talk.' Grace is slacking on your manner lessons."

"Do you deserve a hello?" Truthfully, no. I'd disobeyed his order to come home, a disrespectful defiance to my club president.

"You got me there."

"Where the fuck are you? And don't try to lie to me."

"Wouldn't dream of it, Prez."

"Answer the fucking question, TK. I know you're not with Priest. He called me as soon as you turned back."

"I guess you know where I am, then."

"Better be a good fucking reason for you ignoring not only a call home, but every attempt to connect with you."

I grip the phone, willing him to understand. "I couldn't leave her, Judge."

The other side of the line goes quiet, his heavy

breathing the only thing I hear. "I think you owe me an explanation, son."

"I do. But you, of all people, know what it's like when you find the right woman."

"Fuck, do I know it." Judge would never admit it to us, but Grace changed him, made him better. She had a bit more work cut out for her to change that moody asshole's attitude, but going from zero kids to two hormonal and emotionally damaged teenagers in a blink of an eye, I could see why he's still a moody fucker.

"Cora's my Grace, Judge. Don't ask me why or how, but she is. I don't know what I came up here looking for, but I found it."

"I'm happy for you, TK. Really, man, I am. It's about time you found someone who can keep your ass in line."

"That, she does. You've known me for a long time, seen the shit I've done. My priorities have changed."

"I've seen enough to scar me for life. Shit, we all have."

All I can do is laugh, because he's not wrong. I'd done a lot of shit to get a rise out of my brothers, and for my own personal satisfaction. Shit that I'm now not exactly proud of, but I can't change the past. What I can do is look to the future, shining like a fucking beacon from my bed. My salvation. The redemption I didn't know I needed to find.

"So what's the plan, then?" he asks, never one to beat around the bush. "You stayin'?"

I consider my answer carefully. "I think I am, Judge. Cora's family is here. I can't force her to leave."

"What about the club?"

"I'm no good to you this far away. My only option is to go nomad."

"That's a big decision, TK. We're a family out here. You gonna walk away from that?"

"If I want her, it's the only way. If you knew what she's been through, you'd understand why I can't force her into our lifestyle."

He pauses at that, his unsure tone changing to one of concern. "Enlighten me."

I tell him everything. I tell him about Big Dick raping her and getting her pregnant. I tell him about me and Priest keeping watch over Cora and her family until we could deal with him and make sure they were safe. And then I tell him about what had happened outside of the brewery.

The implications of what I'd done might bring a whole pile of shit down on the club. I know he'll probably be pissed, but I leave nothing out. He listens to everything I say, only letting out the occasional heavy sigh as I talk. "The only reason he's not dead is because Cora stopped me."

"I'd have killed the motherfucker if that were Grace,"

he growls.

"I know, Judge. It would've been easier if I had, considering his affiliation. I haven't seen any blowback yet, but that doesn't mean it's not coming. Hashtag has information on them if it comes to it."

"Of course he does."

"I didn't want to get the club involved. It was personal between him and I."

"If there's blowback from the Screwballs, I'll take care of it. That's a fucking promise."

"I appreciate it, Prez."

Going nomad, there's a chance Judge could cut me off completely. I'd be my own problem, unless another chapter asked me to step in. But with no chapters in this part of the country, those requests would be few and far between.

"Fuck, I saw this going in a different direction," I admit. "I thought Austin was it for me, my home. Turns out, I didn't really know what home was until I met her."

"I hear ya there, kid. Perspectives change when you have a good woman in your life, and leaves you wanting more. Are you ready for this big of a change?"

My pacing on the balcony stops. I look at Cora's sleeping form inside the room and smile. "For her, I'll be ready for anything."

"I'm proud of you, TK. I never thought I'd see the day you'd grow the fuck up, but you've done it."

"I never thought it would either, Judge," I admit with a happy, yet heavy heart.

"It won't be the same without your annoying fucking ass terrorizing the clubhouse."

"Meh. I'll have to come back eventually to get the rest of my shit. There'll be plenty of opportunities to piss you off between now and then, I'm sure." I smile when Judge's laughter flows through the receiver. "Besides," I add, "between V and Priest, I think you'll be fine. The good father has learned from the best."

Judge pauses. "Have you heard from Priest?"

"Not since I left him on the highway outside of Sturgis yesterday. He said something about taking the scenic route since he didn't have my ass to haul away from here, kicking and screaming. He's probably in the middle of nowhere without a phone signal."

"Could be… Or he might just be ignoring me like someone else I know."

"Like I said, he learned from the best. If I hear from him, I'll tell him to call home."

"Appreciate that. I'll let you get back to your girl. See you down the road, brother." He hangs up without letting me get my own goodbye into the conversation. A blessing on his part as a tear rolls down my face.

No one ever said that starting a new chapter in life would be easy, but with Cora, I might just have a chance to make the next one worth the fight.

CORA

"I'M PROUD OF YOU, CORA," my mother says, moving to stand beside me on the back deck, watching TK and my father stack a load of wood. Harrison moves along behind them, picking up small branches and twigs, placing them into a bucket my father has set aside for kindling.

Not that I'm one to ever get upset when my parents are proud of me, but her statement confuses me.

"Why?"

"For a long time, I've watched you go through life, being the best mother you could be to that sweet little boy, and I was proud of you then. But I've also worried that you held everyone but your family at arm's length. I know you had your reasons, but I've always been afraid that you would never release yourself from the guilt you felt about however Harrison came to be, so that you could learn to be loved by the right one."

"I'm still not sure," I admit.

She squeezes my shoulder until I turn and face her. "Even if he's not the right one, you put yourself out there, and for that, I'm proud of you."

I smile on the inside, thinking about just how much of myself I had put out there on the side of the highway the other day.

"Harrison loves him," she continues, redirecting her attention to the men.

"Hey!" Harrison shouts. "Jonas, look at this!"

I watch with a happy heart as my son balances three full-sized pieces of wood in his arms, his knees nearly buckling with the weight as he teeters his way over to the woodpile.

"Good job, little man." TK plucks the wood from Harrison's arms and arranges it the way my father had instructed. "Pretty soon, you'll have muscles as big as mine."

Harrison gapes up at him. "I want muscles like Priest," he declares. "They're way bigger than yours."

My father bursts out with laughter, and my mother and I follow suit. TK just narrows his eyes up at me and shakes his head. "Priest's a wimp," he tells Harrison. "I could take him in a fight any day."

"Whatever," Harrison mutters, rolling his eyes.

After a few minutes, my mother goes back to the kitchen, putting together the finishing touches on our dinner, and I'm left alone to watch the boys work.

TK fits in here. He gets along with my father, and Harrison loves him. But is that enough to justify making this man give up his entire life to be with me?

He'd told me all about what going nomad means, how he would be unaffiliated with any one chapter, but still a member of the Black Hoods. He'd be giving up the brotherhood he has with the Austin chapter, as well as his home and his job.

And what do I have to give up in order for him to do that? Not a single thing, and that's the part that doesn't sit right with me.

What am I clinging to, my parents? My job? My zero close friendships?

My parents want me to be happy, and the rest of it doesn't matter. So why am I insisting this man change it all for me?

That's when I realize that I still don't trust him. That there's a small part of me sure that once he's had his fill of me that he'll go looking elsewhere. And if I had moved to Texas by then, where would that leave me and Jonas?

Maybe my mother spoke too soon when she mentioned how proud she was of my personal growth.

I'm being selfish. I'm still insecure, still keeping him

at arm's length so that I have a safety net in place if we don't work out.

But where's TK's safety net?

He bends over to pick up a pile of wood. Harrison giggles and jumps on his back, his little arms winding around TK's neck as he spins and twirls, pretending that he can't shake him off.

He shouldn't need a safety net. I should be his safety net, and he should be mine.

If I really love this man, I need to show him. I need to completely accept that he loves me for who I am, and stop waiting for him to change his mind.

TK looks up at me and grins, Harrison still dangling from his shoulders. "Tell your mom who the king is."

"I'm the king!" Harrison giggles as TK shakes and jerks, giving my son a bumpy ride that sends his laughter into overdrive.

"Tell her," TK orders.

"I'm the king!" Harrison squeals.

TK bends forward, tipping Harrison off of him and catching him in his arms. He pulls the boy closer, their noses nearly touching.

"Dude, you're making me look bad in front of your mom," TK tells him in a conspiratorial voice.

"My mom has a crush on you. She won't notice that you look bad."

TK closes his eyes and bites back his laugh. "Not the

point, dude. Besides, I kinda have a crush on her too, a big one, so tell her that I'm the king, would ya?"

Harrison considers that for a moment and then turns his gaze to me and yells, "Momma, Jonas says he has a crush on you and that I have to lie to you and tell you that he's the king."

TK meets my gaze over Harrison's head, and the both of us burst into peals of laughter. Even my father is guffawing.

"You're killing me, kid." TK says, cupping his face in his hands and pouting. "You're killing me."

"I don't lie to my mom."

TWATKNOT

SNUGGLING INTO MY CHEST, Cora pulls up the sweat-soaked sheets to cover us both, our hearts still running like a bunch of wild mustangs.

"Fuck, baby."

"Ditto."

I pull my arm around her shoulders and plant a kiss on the top of her head. "Have you thought much about our future?" I ask her.

She goes rigid as she peers up at me. "Like marriage?"

"Shit… I mean, yeah, eventually, but I'm talking about a little sooner than all that."

"What do you mean?" Shifting away from me, she pushes herself up against the headboard and tucks her knees against her chest.

"Like a home? I doubt your parents are going to want

us moving in there, considering how our second set of neighbors were complaining last night."

"Yeah, that's true. Dad might break out that scary spatula again."

"Don't joke about that," I tease. "The man knows how to wield his weapon. I wouldn't stand a chance." We both laugh at the thought of Jim standing there in his *kiss the cook* apron, threatening me with that fucking spatula.

"Yeah, I think I get my attitude from him."

I stifle a laugh. "Not the way he tells it."

"I think it should bother me more that you have had those kinds of talks with my dad when we literally just put a label on our relationship."

"What can I say? I think your dad might've known what we were before we even did."

"Maybe he did."

"About that house. I don't give two shits what kind of house we have so long as you and Harrison are in it. But I know better than to pick it out myself. I want you to get what you want."

She leans her head back and closes her eyes. I don't know whether she's deep in thought or about to fall asleep.

"Are you thinking or sleeping over there?"

"Thinking." Grinning, she opens those pretty brown eyes and looks over at me. "I've never really thought about a house. To be honest, I didn't think I'd ever be able to buy one."

"What do you like?"

"I don't know," she says shyly, tucking a piece of her dark hair behind her ear. "I guess the biggest thing for me would be a big grassy yard for Harrison. He's always wanted a big playset, but my parents didn't have any room for it."

"What else?" I push. "What's important to you?"

"A big kitchen. Space to entertain. Maybe a pool. Is that too much? I'll honestly be happy with whatever we can afford."

"I'm not rich by any means, darlin', but if you want a fucking mansion, I'll figure out a way to get it for you."

She smacks my chest. "What do you think I am? Some bougie bitch?"

"Are you sure you want a pool? Doesn't it get cold here? I don't know shit about either, but if you want one, we'll get it."

"Why would it freeze in Austin?"

Wait, what? My heart leaps. "Did you say Austin?"

"I did." Placing her hand on my chest, she explains, "This isn't your home, TK, and to be honest, it's never been mine either. Not since... you know, but it's where my parents live. I've depended on them a lot, maybe too much, and I think it's time I flew the coop. I'll miss them, but they've always wanted to travel. This is their chance to do that, knowing their daughter is well-cared for."

I gape at her, unable to believe my ears. "You mean it? You'd go to Austin with me?"

"I would. You were willing to sacrifice so much for me and Harrison, and I need to be able to do the same."

"And the club? I know you don't want to live that lifestyle, but I'd still go nomad for you."

"The Black Hoods are a part of you, Jonas. I'm never going to ask you to give up your family for me."

"Say that again."

"Say what again?" she coos, knowing just how much I like hearing my real name on those luscious lips of hers. "Jonas?"

"Fuck, I love hearing you say that," I tell her, pulling her to me for a kiss.

How this woman can make my cock hard just five minutes after fucking her brains out, I'll never understand, but who am I to question God's will?

Cora presses her body against mine and rolls her hips. Fucking hell. I can never get enough of my beautiful Cora. "Keep doing that, we'll never leave this room."

"Maybe that's the plan," she murmurs against my lips.

"I could get down with that plan." She kisses me once

more before pulling away, giving me a smile that makes my heart swell.

"I fucking love you."

"I love you too, Jonas."

"Darlin'," I hiss against her lips. "I'm trying to talk about the future with you, but you're making it really fucking hard."

Sliding her hand between my legs, she glides her palm over my hardening length. "It appears it is… hard."

"Fuuuuck," I groan as she pumps and twists my cock.

"Now," she drawls, climbing to her knees and swinging one over to the far side of my head. "I was kinda hoping you might need a little—"

I don't even let her finish that sentence. I bury my face between her legs and grin as she swirls her hips, riding my tongue with a shaky moan. My girl never has to ask me to eat her sweet pussy.

Chapter 34

CORA

"TO CORA!" Carl bellows, lifting his beer in the air.

"To Cora!" everyone repeats, the sound enough to make me squeal and cover my ears.

The Moose Knuckle is full tonight. I'd thought I was working my final shift, but Carl and a few others made different plans.

Everyone is here, excited and ready to send me off on a new adventure with well wishes and a promise for me to pop by the next time I come to town.

And for the first time, I realize I have more friends than I thought. I'd always wondered why I couldn't find a close friendship like the ones you see in movies or on TV. I'd tried with Rachel and Nicki more times than I can count, but they'd always made sure I never became part of their inner circle.

Which means I'm super surprised to see them both here, drinks in their hands and smiles on their faces.

But everyone else that's here are people I've known my whole life. People that I've gotten to know and love, and will miss dearly.

"You were holding out on me, girl," Greta says, sidling up beside me at the bar. It feels weird to sit on this side while Stella serves me drinks.

"About what?"

"I asked if you were riding that fine piece of man meat, and you didn't tell me shit. What kind of woman does that? Don't you know girls are supposed to share that shit?"

"Well…" I start to laugh. "I wasn't exactly riding him quite yet when you asked me."

She arches her brow. "And now?"

"Oh, now I'm definitely riding him every chance I get."

Greta nods her approval. "Good girl."

And then she's gone, disappearing into the crowd, likely in search of her own baloney pony to ride. *Weirdo.*

"Hey," Rachel squeals, rushing forward with her arms out for a hug. I frown, but allow it, even going so far as to pat her back a couple of times, to be nice. Rachel and I have never hugged in all the history of us knowing each other.

"Hi," Nicki says from beside her, popping her gum

between her teeth as she looks around the room, but never at me.

"I just wanted to say goodbye before you leave tomorrow." She tips her head toward TK on the other side of the bar. "I don't know how you did it, Cora, but your man is fucking gorgeous."

And he's mine, so fuck off, skank. "Thanks."

Nicki sticks her bottom lip out in a pout. "I knew we should've talked to them that night at the concert."

Rachel's eyes bug out at her friend before turning to me with an apologetic smile. "Anyway, I'm glad it worked out for you. I was sure the night I gave you that Xanax you would loosen up a bit and maybe hook up with that biker guy. But then you just kinda dropped off the map for a while, and I was sure you'd stay single forever."

My ears ring as I gape at her, my entire world shifting on its axis. "What did you say?"

She steps closer and raises her voice. "I'm glad it worked out for you," she says slowly, as if she's talking to someone who doesn't understand English.

I push away from the stool. "You drugged me?"

Rachel scoffs and rolls her eyes. "It was years ago, and it was just a little Xanax. What's the big deal?"

I can't move, because if I give my body permission to, even a fraction of a millimeter, I'll punch this woman's teeth down her throat. "What's the big deal?" I repeat. "What's the big deal?"

My voice grows in volume and my blood boils as I poke her in the chest, forcing her back against the wall. "He raped me, Rachel!" I scream, my nose just inches from hers. "He raped me while I was passed out, and that's how I got pregnant with Harrison."

"Oh, fuck," Nicki mutters, but I can't take my eyes off the treacherous bitch in front of me.

"For years, I've blamed myself for what he did to me. I thought I'd done something to make him think I wanted it, but it was you," I seethe.

"Cora," Carl says, his wheelchair moving to get between me and Rachel, at the same time TK comes up behind me and takes my hand.

"Step back, baby."

I feel the tears burning as they spill onto my cheeks. "She drugged me," I whisper, unable to believe my own words.

"I heard." Pulling me away from Rachel, he leads me toward the back door.

"All these years, I thought I'd drank too much and just couldn't remember, but it was her. She did that to me."

The bar goes silent, everyone inside watching the scene unfold before them.

"I know, baby," he says, pulling me to his chest.

"I think you'd better leave," Carl tells Rachel and Nicki, motioning for them to go.

I stare up at TK and shake my head. "What kind of person does that?"

He draws in a deep breath and kisses the top of my head. "A sick one," he replies. "But think about this. What she did was shit. What happened to you was shit. You can't do anything to go back and change it, but you got your boy out of it."

His words wash over me. I have Harrison. And because I have my boy, I wouldn't go back and change it if I could.

"We can deal with that skank anyway you want to, darlin', but for now, let's just enjoy this awesome going away party your friends put together for you. Then, first thing tomorrow morning, we head to Austin."

I hold his stare, using the steadiness he gives me to ground myself. "To Austin."

He kisses the tip of my nose. "Now, go let these people love on you, because after tonight, you're all mine."

Chapter 35

TWATKNOT

THE DRIVE to Texas goes by quickly, despite the many hours we'd spent on the road. With Harrison, we had to make more stops than I would've made on my bike, but I didn't mind. Seeing his face light up at some of the roadside attractions we'd stopped at along the way was worth every extra hour.

The Austin skyline comes into view, just as the sun starts to set. My weary eyes are damn glad to see familiar buildings on the horizon.

It takes another forty minutes until we pull onto the quiet road where my house sits. The brick exterior of my ranch style home stands out against the more traditional two-story cookie cutter homes on the other side of the street in the new subdivision that had been built just last year.

"Is this our house?" Harrison asks excitedly from the back seat of our rented truck.

"It is."

"Whoa!"

Cora reaches out and grabs my arm. "Did you buy this house while we were driving down here?"

"It takes a little bit longer than that to buy a house, darlin'," I tell her, holding in my laughter. "I've lived here for about four years now."

"Alone?"

"Just me. And before you start asking a billion and one questions, I bought it from one of our old club members. He and his wife decided to transfer out east to be closer to their kids. He didn't want the place to sit on the market, so we worked out a deal since it needed some updating. Ten more years of payments, it'll be all ours."

"Baby, I love it."

"Wait till you see the inside. Plenty of room for all that entertaining you want to do." I chuckle when I pull up and see the acre of land surrounding my home filled with motorcycles. "Looks like we'll be doing that sooner rather than later."

I find a spot next to my garage and park. Helping Cora out of the lifted truck, she moves to the back passenger seat to get Harrison from his booster. The bass of rock music booms from the back yard.

"I was hoping to get settled in before we had people over," she admits, adjusting Harrison in her arms.

"That's the funny thing about our club. We're always looking for a good excuse to have a party. If I had to bet, the ladies were behind this one. Come on, let's not keep our unexpected guests waiting."

Cora sets Harrison down, and the little guy takes a hand from each of us.

"Come on, everyone!"

We let him lead us toward the sound of the party. We round the back corner of the house when someone shouts, "welcome home!" The place is decked out. Smoke from two grills that I don't own fog the place up. Patio tables dot the yard with groups of people sitting around them.

Judge waves from the crowd, and with Grace and the kids in tow, they come over to greet us.

"Welcome to Texas," he booms. "Cora, you remember Grace." Grace nods and waves a polite hello. "These are our kids, Kevin and Natalie."

"It's so good to see you again, Grace, and you two as well." Cora smiles, tugging on Harrison's hand with a swing. "This is my son, Harrison. Can you say hi, buddy?"

"Hi," he says bashfully.

"He's normally not shy."

"It's no problem," Grace tells her. "He's been on a

long trip, and all this is new territory for him, and for you too."

"Ain't that the truth," I chime in. "Wasn't expecting a party, Prez."

"You know how the women get when a new lady joins the fray." Grace elbows him in the ribs. "What? It's the truth. Any excuse to throw a party."

"It might be the truth, but you don't have to say it out loud."

"Have I told you how much I like you lately, Grace?" I say, teasing the now scowling Judge. "Ah, there's the grump ass Judge I remember."

The rest of the crowd funnel in to introduce themselves to Cora and Harrison. If Cora was nervous or overwhelmed, she didn't show it. Harrison, on the other hand, took to hiding behind my legs after the three sets of introductions, which I couldn't fault him for. He's probably never been to something like this before.

"You hungry, buddy?" Harrison peeks out from around my leg, bobbing his head. Reaching down, I pick him up and bring him into my arms. "Let's go see what they have to eat."

Cora falls in line behind me as we make our way over to the grills and the tables full of food. "Who's going to eat all this?" she questions, looking down at the large spread in front of her. Plates of ribs, burgers, and steaks take up the majority of the first table. The second has all the sides.

"You have no idea how much these guys can pack away." I look up to see Blair coming from the inside of the house. The fact that my house was unlocked would be something to ask about later, since I sure as hell hadn't left a hideaway key anywhere, nor did anyone else have a copy but me. My gaze falls to her round belly, where her hand rubs around it in a circle. "If this baby is a boy, he's going to eat us out of house and home."

"Cora, this is Blair. She's GP's fiancé."

"Hey there," Blair greets cheerfully. "I wish I could've come up to Sturgis, but GP wouldn't let me ride that long." She rubs her belly, smiling wide. "You'd think as much as he or she kicks, they wanted to go too."

"Where's that old man of yours at, anyway? Judge let him out of the doghouse yet for that little incident while we were gone?"

"Heard about that, huh?"

"Oh yeah. Hash gave me all the dirty details. Good news is, you guys won't be stuck with babysitting duty again."

She barks out a laugh. "That's one way of looking at it. As for that man of mine, he's over there, setting up the karaoke machine." She points over to the other side of the yard where I spy GP and V working on something.

"Karaoke, you say?" Cora beams up at me. "TK loves karaoke."

"The fuck I do."

Blair gasps. "I didn't know that. I didn't even know you could sing."

Cora bursts out laughing. "He can't, and that's the best part."

"I am not singing, Cora. That was a one-time thing, and it ain't ever happenin' again."

Blair looks at Cora, and they both start to giggle.

"Oh yes, you are. I missed most of your last performance, and I want to see the whole thing."

"If I remember correctly, that was your own fault."

"Maybe so, but what better way to welcome me to our new home?"

"No, Cora, I'm not doing it, so drop it."

Cora doesn't drop it, even after I try to distract her by making the rounds to all the tables after we eat, or when Harrison nearly fell asleep with his head on the dinner plate. I'd taken him inside to settle him on my bed before I returned to find Cora sidled up with GP and a binder, looking right at me.

"Picked this one just for you, baby."

"I said no."

"And I said yes. You get up there and sing for me, I'll sing for you later." She gives me a sultry wink. Even as mad as I want to be, the smile on her face makes the sting of embarrassing myself in front of my club hurt just a little less.

"Fine. Give me that fucking microphone." She extends it out to me, and I snatch it from her hand. "This is all for you."

The music starts playing, and I fucking lose it.

"Really, Cora? "I'm Too Sexy"?"

"Sing it, baby! I want to see you shake those hips."

"Yeah, me too," V chimes in, waving a dollar bill in his hand. "Got more of these for you, big guy, if you shake your ass for us."

"Just remember, you asked for this."

The lyrics pop up on the screen, and I belt out the fucking awful song she picked. I cringe at my own voice, but I don't stop. She wanted this, so she's getting it. I dip low, twerking my ass, thrusting my hips, and singing so off key, I hear one of the neighbor's dogs howl. The faces of the crowd are a mix of the ladies laughing at me, and my brothers shaking their heads in disgust. The song finally ends, and I bolt away from that mic, straight to Cora.

She kisses me through the wide smile on her lips.

"You're going to pay for that one," I murmur against her lips.

"Promise?" A challenge if I ever heard of one. I kiss her again before pulling away.

"The second these fuckers leave, and we get Harrison into a room of his own, your ass is mine, lock, stock, and barrel. You have new neighbors to piss off."

Cora smiles, and in that smile, I find my peace, believing that maybe things are finally starting to look up for our club and my life after all.

The party rolls into the wee hours of the night, until the only people left are Judge and me, picking up the discarded beer cans from the yard and putting away what couldn't wait until the next morning. We get the last of it put into the garage before settling into a pair of iron patio chairs I'd inherited with the house. He leans over and hands me a beer from the cooler next to him.

"It's good to be home."

"It's good to have you home, TK." Judge takes a swig of his beer before resting the can on the edge of the chair's arm.

"Never thought I'd miss this place, miss the guys, but fuck, I did. Where was Mom? Didn't see him around."

"He's still dealing with some shit. As much as he wanted to be here, he couldn't make it."

"I get it, family shit. You have Priest on guard duty at the clubhouse for not checking in?"

Judge turns to look at me.

"He still hasn't checked in, TK. No one's heard from

him since he left Sturgis, unless he's gotten back with you."

"I haven't heard shit from him. Tried texting him a couple of times since I called you, but got radio silence. Why didn't you say something before I left? I could've looked out for him on my drive down."

"You said he was taking the scenic route. Unless he's circumventing the globe, he should've been back now, even with that fucking scenic route of his."

"You don't think…? I can't see him taking off. He loves this shit too much, even if he is a boy scout." Priest is many things, but he isn't the kind of guy to abandon his post. Well, again, after the whole priest thing.

"I don't know what to think. Hashtag's been trying to track his phone, but it's been off. I've got a bad feeling about it, TK."

Me too, Judge. Me fucking too.

PRIEST

MY BRAIN THROBS. It feels like a marching band of bass drummers is having drum line practice inside my skull. The thin strip of light from the window above me does little to illuminate the dark, damp room. All I can make out are the four cement walls encasing me, and a makeshift bed that creaks beneath me when I try to move.

"Fuck."

Every muscle in my body screams in agony with any movement I make. It's been days, I think, since I was brought here, maybe longer. Endless cycles of darkness and brief periods of consciousness has my mind all messed up.

My stomach growls. Turning as far as I can on the bed, I retch over the side.

I lie here in pain for what feels like hours before a clunking noise draws my attention to the metal door. I stay quiet as a woman with hot pink braids on either side of her face slips inside the room, then quietly closes the door behind her.

"I brought you something to eat." Taking a few steps forward, she reveals a paper plate with a slice of bread and a smear of peanut butter across it. I try shifting in the cot, but my body is so weak. She moves closer and helps me up before handing me the plate.

My hands shake as I bring the sandwich to my lips. It stings when I swallow, feeling like sandpaper against my throat. I have to cough in an attempt to force it down.

"I'll bring you water next time. They were watching me, so I couldn't bring both."

"Where am I?"

"I can't tell you. If they knew I was in here, they'd kill me."

"Who are they?" I study her pale face, taking in the scars that mark her cheeks and trail down to her collarbone and shoulders. Her left eye is black and blue from a fresh strike that could only be a few days old. "What do they want with me?"

"I don't know that, either."

"Then why are you helping me?"

"Because the only way to survive here is giving them

what they want, and the only way we're getting out is if you're still alive."

————

Read more about Priest's story in Dark Salvation

THE SERIES

Dark Protector

Dark Secret

Dark Guardian

Dark Desires

Dark Destiny

Dark Redemption

Dark Salvation

Dark Seduction

About the Authors

Avelyn Paige is a USA Today and Wall Street Journal bestselling author who writes stories about dirty alpha males and the brave women who love them. She resides in a small town in Indiana with her husband and three fuzzy kids, Jezebel, Cleo, and Asa.

Avelyn spends her days working as a cancer research scientist and her nights sipping moonshine while writing. You can often find her curled up with a good book surrounded by her pets or watching one of her favorite superhero movies for the billionth time. Deadpool is currently her favorite.

––––––––

Want to talk books? Join Avelyn's Facebook group to learn about new releases, future series, and to hang out with other readers.

ALSO BY AVELYN PAIGE

The Heaven's Rejects MC Series

Heaven Sent

Angels and Ashes

Sins of the Father

Absolution

Lies and Illusions

The Dirty Bitches MC Series

Dirty Bitches MC #1

Dirty Bitches MC #2

Dirty Bitches MC #3

Other Books by Avelyn Paige

Girl in a Country Song

Cassie's Court

Geri Glenn writes alpha males. She is a USA Today Bestselling Author, best known for writing motorcycle romance, including the Kings of Korruption MC series. She lives in the Thousand Islands with her two young girls, one big dog and one terrier that thinks he's a Doberman, a hamster, and two guinea pigs whose names she can never remember.

Before she began writing contemporary romance, Geri worked at several different occupations. She's been a pharmacy assistant, a 911 dispatcher, and a caregiver in a nursing home. She can say without a doubt though, that her favorite job is the one she does now–writing romance that leaves an impact.

Want to talk books? Join Geri's Facebook group to learn about new releases, future series, and to hang out with other readers.

ALSO BY GERI GLENN

The Kings of Korruption MC series.

Ryker

Tease

Daniel

Jase

Reaper

Bosco

Korrupted Novellas:

Corrupted Angels

Reinventing Holly

Other Books by Geri Glenn

Dirty Deeds (Satan's Wrath MC)

Hood Rat

Printed in Great Britain
by Amazon

19533307R00142